Kidnapped -by- River Rats

Trailblazer Books

HISTORIC CHARACTERS	TITLE
Gladys Aylward	Flight of the Fugitives
Mary McLeod Bethune	Defeat of the Ghost Riders
William & Catherine Booth	Kidnapped by River Rats
Charles Loring Brace	Roundup of the Street Rovers
William Bradford	The Mayflower Secret
John Bunyan	Traitor in the Tower
Amy Carmichael	The Hidden Jewel
Peter Cartwright	Abandoned on the Wild Frontier
Maude Cary	Risking the Forbidden Game
George Washington Carver	The Forty-Acre Swindle
Frederick Douglass	Caught in the Rebel Camp
Elizabeth Fry	The Thieves of Tyburn Square
Chief Spokane Garry	Exiled to the Red River
Barbrooke Grubb	Ambushed in Jaguar Swamp
Jonathan & Rosalind Goforth	Mask of the Wolf Boy
Sheldon Jackson	The Gold Miners' Rescue
Adoniram & Ann Judson	Imprisoned in the Golden City
Festo Kivengere	Assassins in the Cathedral
David Livingstone	Escape From the Slave Traders
Martin Luther	Spy for the Night Riders
Dwight L. Moody	Danger on the Flying Trapeze
Lottie Moon	Drawn by a China Moon
Samuel Morris	Quest for the Lost Prince
George Müller	The Bandit of Ashley Downs
John Newton	The Runaway's Revenge
Florence Nightingale	The Drummer Boy's Battle
John G. Paton	Sinking the Dayspring
William Penn	Hostage on the Nighthawk
Joy Ridderhof	Race for the Record
Nate Saint	The Fate of the Yellow Woodbee
Rómulo Sauñe	Blinded by the Shining Path
William Seymour	Journey to the End of the Earth
Menno Simons	The Betrayer's Fortune
Mary Slessor	Trial by Poison
Hudson Taylor	Shanghaied to China
Harriet Tubman	Listen for the Whippoorwill
William Tyndale	The Queen's Smuggler
John Wesley	The Chimney Sweep's Ransom
Marcus & Narcissa Whitman	Attack in the Rye Grass
David Zeisberger	The Warrior's Challenge

Kidnapped –by– River Rats

Dave & Neta Jackson

Illustrated by Julian Jackson

CASTLE ROCK CREATIVE
Evanston, Illinois 60202

Published by Castle Rock Creative, Inc.
Evanston, Illinois 60202

Previously published by
Bethany House, a division of
Baker Publishing Group

Unless otherwise noted, all Scripture quotations are from the King James Version of the Bible

Inside illustrations by Julian Jackson
Cover illustration by Catherine Reishus McLaughlin

ISBN: 978-1-939445-03-2

Printed in the United States of America

For a complete listing of
books by Dave and Neta Jackson visit
www.daveneta.com
www.trailblazerbooks.com

William and Catherine Booth, Charlie Fry and his Hallelujah Band, and George Scott Railton and the seven Hallelujah Lasses commissioned to "invade" New York were real people. All other characters are fictional. However, the situations presented in this story accurately portray the conditions of many children in London in the 1880s as well as the life and ministry of the Salvation Army.

Dave and Neta Jackson, husband and wife writing team, are the authors or coauthors of more than 120 books that have sold over 2.5 million copies. They are best known for the 40-volume Trailblazer Books series for young readers and the Hero Tales series for families. Adults love their Yada Yada Prayer Group series, House of Hope series, Harry Bentley series, and Windy City Neighbors series along with numerous nonfiction books. They make their home in the Chicago area. Find out more about them at www.daveneta.com.

CONTENTS

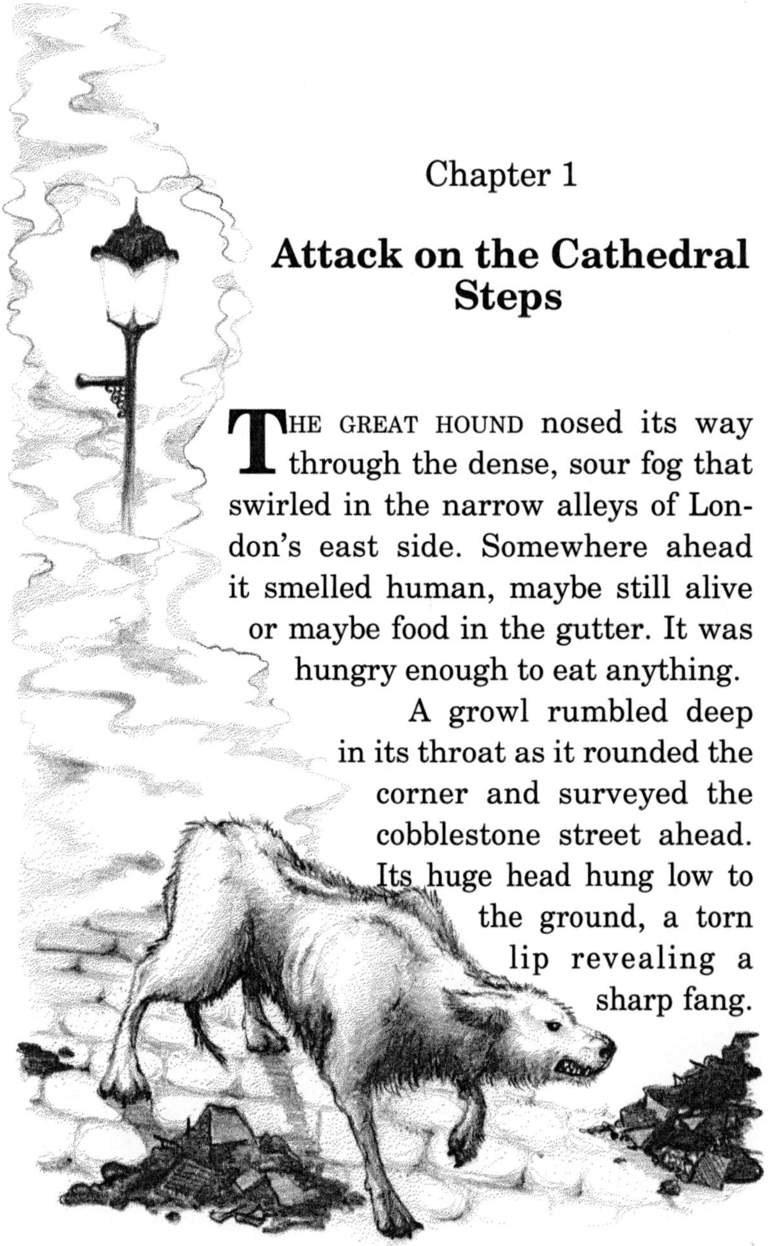

Chapter 1

Attack on the Cathedral Steps

THE GREAT HOUND nosed its way through the dense, sour fog that swirled in the narrow alleys of London's east side. Somewhere ahead it smelled human, maybe still alive or maybe food in the gutter. It was hungry enough to eat anything.

A growl rumbled deep in its throat as it rounded the corner and surveyed the cobblestone street ahead. Its huge head hung low to the ground, a torn lip revealing a sharp fang.

Coarse, gray hair spiked along the ridge of its back. The lone gas light in front of Saint Paul's Cathedral cast a greenish glow through the mist. No one there.

Or was there? Deep in the shadows of the side door to the cathedral lay a black heap. The dog approached quietly, sniffing the heavy air. No death here . . . but maybe there would be something to eat just the same.

Jack Crumpton came awake slowly. Why was Mama pulling on his night shirt? Why was his bed so hard? Why was he so cold?

And then it all came back to him. He wasn't in bed . . . Mama was dead, and he and Amy were homeless on the streets of London.

He rolled over with a start. There, snarling and pulling on the sleeve of his coat, stood the biggest wolf-dog he'd ever seen. Jack grabbed for his stick. It was caught under Amy. He pulled it free and swung it at the beast's immense head. The creature ducked the blow without loosening his bite on the coat.

Just then Amy sat up and screamed, "Don't let him have it, Jack! The biscuits in your pocket are our last food."

With one hand Jack pulled with all his might on his coat. With the other he swung his stick toward the dog's nose. This time the stout stick landed with a sharp whack. The brute yelped and made one more desperate lunge backwards, its ugly fangs still embedded in the sleeve of Jack's old coat. The strength of the beast pulled Jack over and he rolled down the steps. But he wouldn't give up his coat.

And then with a sickening rip, the sleeve tore free, and the dog made off into the gloom with Jack's sleeve flapping around its head like a neck scarf in a winter blow.

Jack rose slowly to his knees on the grimy street and tried to inspect his coat by the dim glow of the nearby street light. Safely in its pocket there remained two small hunks of bread no bigger than his fists.

"You all right?" asked Amy as she came down to help him up.

"Yeah, but he got me sleeve. Guess I'll have one cold arm come winter."

"Don't worry, Jack. By then we'll find Uncle Sedgwick, and he'll surely take us in."

"I hope so," Jack said as he followed his older sister back up the steps to huddle in the skimpy shelter of the doorway to the great cathedral. Amy shared her shawl with him, wrapping the garment that their mother had knitted around the both of them. In the dim light its beautiful light and dark greens looked like gray and black, but it was still just as warm.

London had been strange and unfriendly to the two children. They had come to the city a few weeks earlier with their mother after their father had died in a coal mine accident. Mama hoped to find her brother Sedgwick Masters, a successful tailor. But in London in the fall of 1881, it wasn't so easy to track someone down if you weren't sure of his address. Mama's cough seemed worse after the damp, two-day journey to London, so they found lodging where the landlady charged two shillings per night for an unheated gable room at the back of a dreary house.

The next day, Mother was too ill to look for Uncle Sedgwick. She soon got so sick that the children didn't dare leave her side. They took turns going out to find a penny's worth of bread or some vegetables or broth and bringing it back to Mama. And each day Mrs. Witherspoon, the landlady, came pounding on the door demanding the rent until in one week's time almost all their money was gone.

"You can't stay here without paying your rent," the old landlady had said gruffly. Jack thought her face looked like a prune.

"We'll pay," promised Mother, and then fell into a great fit of coughing that brought up more blood. When she finally got her breath back, she said, "Just give me a chance to get well and find my brother, Sedgwick Masters, the tailor."

"I've never heard of any tailor by that name. Besides, you got consumption, woman. You ain't never gonna get well."

The old woman had been right. Four days later Mother Crumpton died in her sleep.

When Witherspoon came for the rent the next morning, she started shrieking twice as loud as the children had cried during the night. "I told you! I told you she'd never make it. Now what am I going to do?

What am I going to do? You two young'uns get out of here. I should never have let this room out to you in the first place." She paced back and forth wringing her hands. "What am I ever going to do?" Then she looked at the children again: "Get out! Get out, I told you."

"But we can't go—that's our mama," protested Amy.

"Was . . . was. She was your mama. She ain't no more. This here's just a body that I'm going to have to pay to have taken away. And this room ain't yours any more, so get out!"

Fighting back the tears, Jack went over and struggled with the trunk that held all their belongings. He was strong for twelve years of age, and Amy, who was just two years older, could put in a full day's work. But they would have done well to get the trunk down the stairs, let alone carry it any distance through London's narrow, busy streets.

"You can just leave that right there," growled old lady Witherspoon. "I'll hold it as collateral 'til you pay up. You owe me five days rent plus whatever it costs to have this body taken away. Until you pay up, you can just leave that trunk right here. Now go find that rich uncle of yours, if you got one."

The two children, numb with grief, had wandered aimlessly around London's lower east side until they fell asleep in the doorway of the great cathedral. Now wide awake, their hearts beating loudly as they peered into the darkness, fearful that the beast would return, Amy resolved, "Tomorrow, Jack. Tomorrow we'll go find Uncle Sedgwick."

They arranged their coats over themselves as they cuddled together. Jack listened to the night as the distant wail of a baby's cry drifted through the dense fog.

Yes, tomorrow they had to find Uncle Sedgwick.

Chapter 2

Blood and Fire

When Jack awoke in the morning, his sister was already sitting up watching the hustle and bustle of the street. Jack rubbed his eyes and turned over to see what drew her attention.

They had slept late. The sun had already burned off most of the fog, leaving a bright haze overhead. Jack looked up. There was a hazy circle around the sun; must mean rain.

The street was full of people. A fat woman waddled by carrying a large basket of laundry. She was so fat that she seemed to have to work very hard just to get where she was going. "Hold on ta me skirts," she barked at three apple-faced children coming on behind her, each one a smaller copy of the mother.

A man pulled a creaking two-wheeled cart piled high with lumps of coal. "I miss Pa," Jack said as tears came to his eyes. He pulled his cap lower. Straight brown hair poked out all around. His hair was the same color as his mother's had been. Amy, however, had her father's hair—red and curly, but not so red as to look orange and not so curly as to be frizzy. For a sister, she could look very pretty, Jack sometimes thought. Today, however, smears of dirt trailed across her forehead and down one cheek. Her hair was tousled, her clothes a mess. Mother would never have let Amy go out looking like that. But now she was gone, and they were alone, so alone.

"What you lookin' at?" Amy asked. "Give me one of those biscuits."

Jack dug in his pocket and took out the hunks of stale bread. He handed one to Amy and stuck the other in his teeth as he examined his coat with its missing sleeve. He ought to go search for it. There was a good chance the dog dropped it once it realized it held nothing to eat.

"You think that dog would have eaten us last night?" he asked Amy.

"I doubt it. Who ever heard of a dog eating a person? It's not like we were sheep and it was a wolf."

"Dogs go bad and kill sheep sometimes," said Jack. "Besides, that one last night looked half-wolf."

"That it did. I've never seen such an ugly thing. I did once hear of dogs eating dead people during a famine."

Just then Jack heard the most peculiar sound. It was the high pitched sound of a flute and the deep thump, thump, thump of a drum. He stuffed the rest of the biscuit in his mouth and looked down the street. Coming around the corner about one street away was a small parade. Each person was in a uniform; most carried some kind of a band instrument, and one held high a brightly colored flag, but it was not the familiar British Union Jack.

"You think they're bobbies?" asked Jack, ready to run.

"Policemen don't march around with a band," said Amy. "Otherwise how would they ever catch any crooks?"

The troop continued marching up the narrow street beside the cathedral. Small children, chickens, and cats scampered to the side to get out of the way. Then, right at the bottom of the steps, a tall, wiry-haired man with a bushy, gray beard and a black top hat shouted a command, and the troop stopped and turned like a machine toward Amy and Jack.

"They *are* bobbies," yelled Jack as he grabbed his sister's hand and tried to make a break for it.

"Hold on there, lad," said the man with the big beard as he easily reached out and caught Jack's arm. "Where are you off to so fast?"

"We ain't done nothin'," stammered Jack. "We just . . . I mean, sir, we are just looking for our uncle." Jack squirmed to get free.

"Listen, lad, we're not the police, and we're not after anything more than your soul. But I do want to talk to you. So will you hold still a minute?"

After my soul? thought Jack. *Who could be after my soul other than God or the devil?* Jack had only occasionally gone to church, but he wasn't about to let anyone get his soul. On the other hand, you can't just grab a body's soul, or could you? Jack stood still, and the man's iron grip loosened on his arm.

The man took off his top hat and stooped down with his hands on his knees until he was on eye level with Jack. The man's nose was large and somewhat hooked. His gray eyes shone like polished steel, deep-set under two eyebrows that were not shaped the same. The right one arched high while the left one sloped giving him a skeptical expression.

"So, where do you two live?" he commanded. His

wiry beard jutted out and bobbed with each word, carefully pronounced with military precision.

"We live . . . ," began Jack.

"We live with our Uncle Sedgwick," finished Amy with authority.

"I see." The man cocked his head and examined Amy. "But you don't know where he is . . . , and so you must 'look' for him. Is that it?" Both children nodded. "A likely story, indeed," said the man.

"General, come now," interrupted a woman who stepped forward. "Can't you see that these children are scared to death? I'm Catherine Booth, children," beamed the woman with a warm smile. She wore a dark blue bonnet tied under her chin by a broad red ribbon. "And this man, who would love to take you captive, is none other than my husband, General William Booth of the Salvation Army."

It was only then that Jack realized that the troop was made up almost equally by men and women. While the women wore long dresses, their uniform was very military looking. And as for the men, they did look like soldiers on dress parade with sharply cut, dark blue uniforms and small brimmed caps with shiny metal crests on the front. The general was dressed the same except for his top hat and slightly different insignia on his uniform. Then Jack noticed that on the collar of each person there was a highly polished, brass letter S.

While Mrs. Booth talked, the other members of the troop set up the flag and the drum and prepared to play right on the steps of Saint Paul's Cathedral. A chill ran through Jack's body as a slight breeze waved the flag. He didn't read too well, but he easily made out the words "Blood and Fire" inscribed above a cross, two crossed swords, and again the letter S. "Blood and Fire" . . . "Blood and Fire" . . . what could it mean?

Mrs. Booth concluded her introduction by inviting the children to stay and listen to the music. Her face was solemn but her eyes were smiling.

"I think we'd better be going," said Amy as she pulled Jack down the steps and away from this strange army. "Jack, she *said* that the general wants to take us captive," whispered Amy when Jack tried to squirm away.

The children spent all that morning walking the streets of East London looking for their uncle. Time and again they would race forward when they saw a sign indicating a tailor's shop. But when they got close, it always had someone else's name on it.

Once when they were getting a drink of water from a public fountain, Amy said, "Maybe we ought to be going inside and asking, even though his name's not on the sign. Maybe his shop is in someone else's name."

"That means we have to go back and check each one we've been to," moaned Jack.

"But it might speed up our search," said Amy. "One tailor ought to know the others. If they are in the same business, someone is bound to know him, and can direct us to the right shop."

In the third shop they entered, a skinny old man as crooked as a dried-out oak limb glanced up over the top of his spectacles and said, "Sedgwick Masters, eh? What'cha want him for?"

"He's our uncle, and we're trying to find him," said Amy.

"Well, I don't know where he is," said the old man, returning to his sewing, "and I don't care to know, either."

"Why not?" asked Jack.

"'Cause the last time I heard of him was when he stole two of my best customers."

The children stared as the man put a handful of pins in his mouth. Finally Amy said, "But you have seen him, then?"

"Didn't say I'd seen him," mumbled the tailor as he took one pin after another from his mouth as fast as a dog scratches fleas and stuck them in the garment he was sewing. "Actually, I never laid eyes on the man."

"But you gotta know where he is if your customers went to him," persisted Amy.

"Listen here, young lady, I don't gotta know nothin'. When one of my customers came back to me, I was grateful. I didn't pry into why he had left or why he came back."

Jack and Amy walked to the door in despair. Then suddenly Jack turned back. "Wait," he said. "Who were those people, the customers of yours who went to our Uncle Sedgwick? Where are they now? Maybe they know where our uncle is."

"Like I said, only one came back. He was that dandy, Filbert. Wanted me to make him three new suits so he could impress the ladies of Europe. Last I heard, he'd set sail for France. Was going to tour the Continent for 'his cultural enrichment,' he said. I haven't seen him since."

"Who was the other person," said Jack, "the one who didn't come back?"

"Well, now, I do know that she's still around. But she's never come back to me, so maybe she's still using Masters. Who knows?"

"But who was she?" persisted Jack.

"Oh, she's the wife of that general, or so-called general. Booth, Catherine Booth, was her name. They're the ones who started that Salvation Army. They march around here all the time." The tailor looked up at Jack and added, "Say, boy, you better get your jacket fixed. You're missing a sleeve there."

Chapter 3

Caught for a Thief

AMY AND JACK LEFT the tailor's shop in high spirits. Their uncle couldn't be far, and now they knew someone who could lead them to him.

"But, Amy," said Jack, "that woman said the general wanted to take us captive. What if he does?"

"We can't let him," said Amy. "We'll have to find them when they're not together and ask her then."

They headed back toward the cathedral. It was a long walk, and it was getting late in the afternoon. As they hiked along, Jack noticed a most wonderful smell. He looked up, and there in the window of a building that was built right out to the street sat two steaming pies. Jack stopped, and that caused Amy to stop and look up too. "They're chicken pies, just like Mom makes," said Amy.

Jack's stomach growled and suddenly ached. The children were getting very hungry, not having had anything to eat all day except one hard biscuit early that morning, but Jack's stomach hurt from more than hunger. "They're just like Mom *made. Made,* Amy, not *'makes.'* Mother can't make pies anymore.

Remember? It's just like old lady Witherspoon said, Mom's dead." He stomped off down the street, keeping his head turned away so Amy wouldn't see the tears that swam in his eyes.

"Jack, wait." Amy caught up to him. "I didn't mean anything. Those pies just made me think about Mom; that's all. I miss her too, you know."

"Yeah, I know," he mumbled. "It's just that I wish she hadn't left us. It ain't fair; now we're all alone, and I'm starving."

"Don't be angry, Jack. It wasn't her fault. We just gotta hang together and find Uncle Sedgwick. Then we can get something to eat."

"But what if we never find him?"

"We will; we will."

They rounded a corner and came to a street market. Jack's mouth watered when he looked at the bright red apples in a grocery stall. *Just one bite, just one bite would taste so good,* he thought. The grocer was looking the other way, helping a customer. Suddenly Jack grabbed two apples, one for himself and one for Amy, and tried to put them into his pockets. But the apples were so big that they wouldn't fit. While he was struggling, the grocer turned around and saw him.

"Hey, you little brat," he yelled. "Put them back."

In fright Jack turned and started to run. "Amy, come on."

For a moment Amy was confused, but when she saw the grocer lunge around the end of his table with his cane raised high, she started running after Jack fast enough.

"Stop, thief. Stop, thief," yelled the grocer as they dodged between the other stalls in the street market. Jack turned down an alley, an apple clutched in each hand, and Amy was right behind him. The cobble stones of the alley were rough, and garbage and puddles of sewage made it slick. Jack looked back to see the grocer hot on their heels.

Suddenly Amy screamed, and Jack heard a loud crash. When he looked back, a rain barrel had tipped over into the center of the alley and had broken open.

Water was flooding everywhere. Amy was on the ground in the middle of it. Just then the grocer skidded to a stop above her and grabbed her by her hair. He raised his cane.

"No," yelled Jack and raised his two apples high so the man could see them. "Don't hit my sister."

"You bring them apples back to me, then, you little tea-leaf."

Jack approached the grocer. The man's face was purple, and he was breathing hard, but he hadn't let go of Amy's hair. Jack put both apples in one hand—they were almost too big to hold that way—and came closer, holding them out to the man. Suddenly the cane whistled through the air and came crashing down on Jack's hand and wrist. One apple exploded; the other went flying across the alley. Jack felt more pain shoot up his arm than he had ever known in his life. "That'll teach you ta thieve from me, you little brats. Every day, robbing me blind. It's got so a man can't make a livin' any more." And with that the man turned and lumbered back up the alley.

Jack realized that he was crying. He didn't want to cry; he wanted to be brave for Amy. But he couldn't help it. A great red welt was growing across his wrist, and his hand felt like he'd never use it again. Then Jack noticed that Amy was crying too. Her clothes were wet, and she was holding her ankle. "What's wrong," said Jack through his sobs.

"I think I hurt my ankle," she said.

"Can you stand up?" Jack asked.

"I don't know. I think it's really hurt. But what about your hand?"

Jack held it out and tried to move his fingers. At least they did move, but the pain throbbed harder than ever. "I think it's okay," he said, not at all sure that was so.

"Here, help me up," said Amy.

Jack offered his other hand to help her. Amy stood up using Jack for balance, keeping her right foot off the ground. Slowly she put it down and tried one feeble step, but the moment she put weight on it, she gave a little cry and almost fell again. "I think it's really hurt, Jack."

"What're we gonna do?"

"I don't know. Maybe it's just twisted. Here, let me lean on you."

The two hobbled back down the alley as evening turned the shadows to blue, purple, then gray. "Wait a minute," said Jack. "Grab hold of the corner of the building." Then he ran back down the alley searching for something.

In a few minutes he returned. "Here," he said as he held out the badly bruised apple that had not been totally smashed by the grocer's cane. "I know it isn't ours, and I shouldn't have taken it. I'm sorry about that, 'specially because of your foot. But I guess the grocer didn't want it. At least he didn't take it back, and we need something to eat. Want a bite?" He rubbed it on his pants to wipe off the alley's grime.

Amy took a bite, then held onto Jack's shoulder as they limped off down the street sharing the apple.

Chapter 4

The Cave in the City

IT WAS NEARLY DARK. The lamplighter was lighting the lamps on each post.

"Jack, I don't know where we are. I don't know where the cathedral is any more."

"Neither do I," said Jack. "But there's something different up ahead. It looks like the street ends. But then there's nothing."

As they approached, they found that the street butted into another one that went along the side of a great river. On the river moved large barges, barely visible in the dark except that some had a lantern on deck. On the other side of the river down farther were three ships tied up. The tall masts and rigging of these sailing ships made a lacy silhouette against the last pale light in the sky.

"I don't think I can walk any more," said Amy. "My foot's hurtin' something fierce. I wish Mother were here. She would know what to do." The two made their way out of the street just as a coach and four horses raced past, the wheels and hooves clattering on the rough cobblestones. Amy leaned on the wall for support. Jack gazed at the shiny black water below.

"There's something down there," Jack muttered almost to himself. "I'm climbing down."

"Wait," said Amy as she reached for her brother, but he was already scrambling over the wall, lowering himself to the river. Then she, too, noticed it. Right below them the water did not come all the way to the wall. There was a little sandy beach not much wider than what a person could walk on.

Jack walked along it toward a nearby bridge. At the base of the pillar supporting the end of the bridge the little stretch of sand was replaced by large rough rocks. Jack's fingers found small handholds in the cracks between the stones of the pillar, and he hung on as he carefully inched his way around the pillar, stepping from one slippery rock to the next. There, under the end of the bridge was a small cave. It actually extended ten or twelve feet back under the street above. The floor of the cave was sandy, and when one got away from the river a ways, it was pretty dry. A large limb of a tree and other pieces of driftwood had piled up along one side. There was even a packing box and a broken bucket.

Something scurried across the sand and into the pile of driftwood. Maybe it was a cat . . . or a rat. But if it was a rat, it was the biggest rat Jack had ever seen. Jack reached down and picked up a stone. "Show your head just one time," Jack threatened. When nothing moved, he cut loose with a wicked sling anyway and the stone cracked against the old

bucket. Still nothing came out. Jack picked up a second stone and moved toward the back of the cave, ever watchful of the pile of trash. But the back of the cave was so dark that he could only sense its general location. He didn't *think* there was anything else lurking back there, but he wasn't going back there by himself to find out.

"Jack! Jack! What are you doing?"

Jack could just hear his sister's voice. He climbed back around the pillar and looked up at her. The evening gloom made her face barely visible. "There's a cave down here!" Jack said.

"So?"

"This is great! Come on down."

"Jack, why would I want to climb down there to explore an old cave? We don't even have a place to sleep tonight."

"Why not in this cave? At least if it rained, we wouldn't get wet. There's some wood down here. We could even light a fire."

Amy groaned. "Jack, sometimes I don't know what to do with you. Don't you realize that my ankle is hurt? I could never climb down there."

"Yes you could. It's not far."

Amy stood there looking at him, then out across the river, then back across the street into the part of London where they'd spent the day looking without luck for their uncle. Finally she turned back to Jack. "Okay. But you've got to help me get down. My ankle is swelling up bigger and bigger."

In a few minutes both children were standing together on the narrow strip of sand at the river's edge. The night sounds of the big city were cut off from them, and all they could hear was the gentle ding, ding, ding of the bell from the river buoy up near where the ships were docked.

Jack held Amy's arm as she inched herself around the pillar. Once her foot slipped on the rough rocks below and she turned her ankle again. She cried out, then caught her breath. He could see pain etched on her face.

"Here we are," Jack said encouragingly.

Amy hobbled across the sand toward the back of the cave. "It's dry now. But what happens if it rains and the river level rises. We'd be flooded out. In fact, how would we even get out?"

Jack shrugged, then realized that it was too dark in the cave for Amy to see his gesture. "Here, let's make a fire," he said as he drew a few of the smaller sticks from the pile of driftwood and trash. He tried not to think of the animal that had so recently run into that pile.

"How are we going to light a fire, Jack? We don't have any matches. There's no way we can light a fire down here."

"Maybe we could go borrow some coals from someone's hearth," offered Jack.

"Sure, just walk up to one of those pubs along the riverfront and say, 'Could we please have some live coals. We ain't got no place to live and we're camping under the bridge.' If we did that, one of those drunken sailors would throw us in the river."

Jack continued breaking sticks and laying them for a fire. There had to be a way; there just had to be.

"Jack! I know. Take a little stick and climb up one of the street light poles. Stick it in there just like the lamplighter does. But instead of lighting the lamp, you can light your stick to bring back for some fire."

It was a great idea. Jack found a small, dry stick in the pile of trash and left the little cave. He climbed the wall and ran down the street to the nearest lamp. But climbing the pole wasn't as easy as it looked. It

took him three tries before he made it. Then clinging carefully to the pole, he put his stick into the little hole and touched the flame. It flared brightly, and he slid down the pole.

The stick was burning fast. Jack ran down the dark street and scrambled over the wall and dropped to the sand below. But the fall through the air blew out the flame. He stood there by the black river with only a glowing ember in his hand. Carefully he blew on it to get a weak flame to return. It glowed brightly for a moment, but then went out completely.

"Amy, get me another stick—a little longer, and make sure it's dry. This one went out."

In a few moments Amy handed another stick around the pillar so that neither child had to navigate the slippery rocks. Jack climbed back up the wall. He was getting to know where the good hand and foot holds were now, even in the dark.

This time when he returned with the burning stick he was careful not to shake his hand as he dropped the last few feet to the ground. The flame held.

Back in the cave he held it to the little pile of wood he had made. Some of the smallest splinters lit easily, but they also burned down quickly. As the little flames on the sticks grew smaller and smaller, both children huddled close and blew gently, adding one twig at a time. Finally, when they thought they were going to be plunged back into darkness, some new sticks caught and the fire began to grow.

They fed it with new wood and smiled as it crackled cheerily. At last they began to feel warm as they cuddled together on the sand at the back of the river cave.

Chapter 5

River Rats

IT WAS DRIZZLING when the children awoke in the morning. They sat up and looked out into the river. A riverboat was pulling slowly upstream; two men worked steadily on the oars to move it against the current. The open boat was piled high with potatoes and cabbages—going to market, no doubt.

"Wish I could have one of them," said Jack. "I'm starving."

In the distance they could see several other boats on the water—people starting their day to the sour smell of coal smoke in the London air.

"Oh, no. Our fire's gone out," moaned Amy as she pulled her shawl around her shoulders. "And the street lamps will have been put out by now. We can't even get another light until tonight."

"It's not my fault," said Jack. "You could have gotten up in the night and put on more wood yourself. There's plenty of it."

"I didn't say it was your fault. I just said we don't have a fire."

"It sounded like you were blaming me," complained Jack.

"Well, I wasn't. So what's the matter with you this morning?"

"I'm just hungry," said Jack. Tears came to his eyes. "And I want Mama. Why'd she have to die?"

Amy put her arms around him, and together the two children cried. Finally Amy sniffed and wiped her face with her shawl. "But we can't give up, Jack. We just can't."

"But what are we going to do?"

"This morning you have to go find that Salvation Army woman. What was her name?"

"You mean the one the tailor said was Uncle Sedgwick's customer? Booth something, wasn't it?"

"Yes. Booth, Catherine Booth. You have to go find her, Jack. Catherine Booth, don't forget that name."

"But why not you?"

In answer, Amy stuck out her foot and pointed to her ankle. "I really can't walk, Jack. There's no way I can wander around the city until I get better."

"What about the river?" said Jack. "What if this rain makes it rise and floods you out like you said?"

"It's not rising yet. Look at those rocks, the water's even lower." She nodded over to the piling around which they had to climb every time they came into the cave. "You know, unless there is a real big rain or spring floods, I think the only thing that changes the water level in this river is the tide."

Jack looked suspiciously at the pile of trash. "The tide? But that comes from the sea every day, twice a day. We've already been here one whole night, and there hasn't been any high tide."

"No. I'm talking about big tides, the kind that come once a month. Maybe they come up the river this far. I don't know."

"Yeah, maybe that's how all this junk got here. It floated here sometime when the river was high, high enough to come up into this very cave. And we don't know when that's going to happen."

"Well, it's not going to happen today," said Amy. "I'll tell you what, you go looking for Catherine Booth, and if it starts raining hard, you can come back here and help me out."

That seemed to satisfy Jack, and he got up to leave.

Part way out into the river there was another set of pillars holding up the huge bridge. Up near the top in the shadows of the beams Jack noticed movement. He looked closely and then realized what it was. A rat was crawling along the beam, possibly the very one that had hid in their pile of driftwood the night before. Jack stooped down and found three stones in the sand. Carefully he eased over to the side of the cave to get a better angle. The rat was in full view now, stopping every few moments and looking around.

Suddenly Jack let fly with a rough, oblong stone. It was a long throw, but Jack was a good shot. The stone whizzed just over the rat's head. The ugly creature bounded forward a few feet then stopped and looked around, its round rump high and its

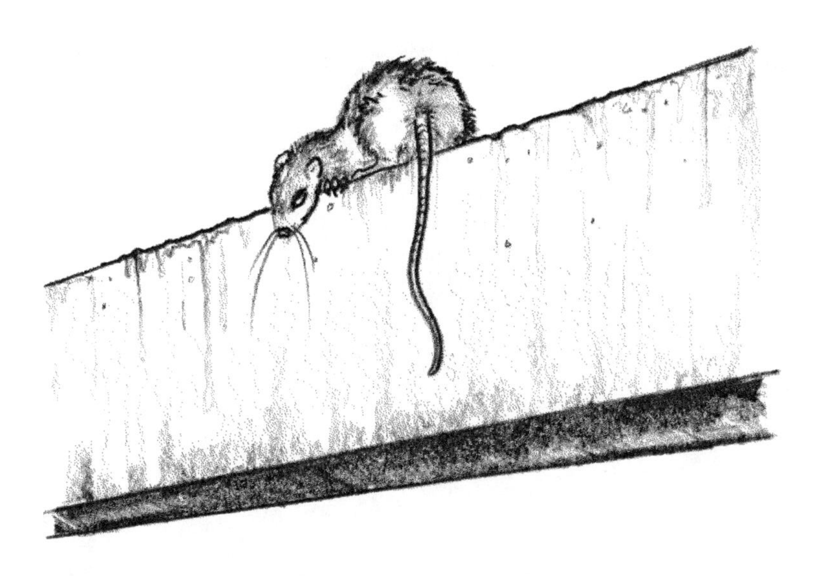

beady eyes shining. Apparently the rat was uncertain what had happened or where its enemy was. That moment of hesitation was all Jack needed. He took aim and flung a second stone with all his might. It sailed through the air and found its mark, hitting with a thud that knocked the rat off the beam and into the river.

"You got him, Jack."

"Yeah." Jack stared at the place where the rat had splashed into the water. In a few moments something floated to the surface and drifted lifelessly down stream. "Yeah, I got him good." In his excitement, Jack flung his third rock out over the river in the general direction of where the rat had been. But because he hadn't aimed, the stone flew beyond the pillar and landed on the front of a boat that had just nosed out from behind the pillar.

"Hey, what's the big idea?" yelled a burly voice as a huge sailor stood up in the boat. His partner continued rowing. "What you brats trying to do? You want to kill someone? I've a mind to come in there and thrash the both of you."

"We didn't mean to," answered Amy.

"Hey, Rodney," said the one still at the oars. "It's a girl."

"Yeah, and just about the right age too. But we got to get back to the ship. We'll take care of this later." Then he yelled again at Amy and Jack, "You throw any more rocks at us, and I'll bust your heads."

"We won't," said Jack.

"You bet you won't, and we'll be back to see that you don't too." They laughed with a roar as the big man sat down clumsily and took up his oars. Soon they were far down the river.

"That was a close one," said Jack. "I almost got two river rats." And he laughed.

"Don't joke about it, Jack. Those were evil men."

"You don't think they will be back, do you Amy?"

"Who knows. They probably go back and forth from their ship every day when they are in port. We'll just have to attract no more attention. Now you go on, Jack. See if you can find that Booth lady."

"But I'm starving, Amy. When are we going to get something to eat?"

"I don't know. I'm hungry too. Maybe you can ask someone to give you some bread when you are out."

"Yeah, maybe so. I'll bring you back something," said Jack as he worked his way around the rocks at the bottom of the piling. "I promise that I'll get you something."

Chapter 6

Three Good Hits

By the time Jack had climbed up to the street, the drizzle had stopped, for which he was very grateful. The streets were full of people, and no one seemed to pay any attention to the young boy climbing over the wall along the edge of the River Thames.

Jack looked all morning for the Salvation Army. He found the church where he and Amy had spent the night, but they weren't there. He asked people on the street where they were. "Oh, they're around; they're around here every day somewhere," a boy about Jack's age told him. "Why, you looking to throw a little mud?" the boy asked.

"No. Why would I throw mud?" Jack said.

"Beats selling papers," the boy shrugged as he ran off.

Jack didn't understand what he was talking about. Why would throwing mud beat selling papers?

The smell of baking bread caught Jack's attention. It was coming from a bakery with rolls and loaves of bread in every shape and size in the window. There was black bread, brown bread, and even white bread. His mouth watered as he looked through the window, and he remembered his promise to bring Amy something to eat.

An idea struck him, and he ran down the street to the next corner. He turned and ran on until he found a little alley that led him to the back of the bakery shop. He pounded on the door until a bald man with bushy black eyebrows opened the door.

"Yeah, what'cha want?"

"Sorry to bother you, sir. But I was wonderin' if I could earn a loaf of bread?"

"Away with you. We got too many beggars around here already."

"I ain't no beggar, sir. I was wantin' to work for it. Any old job will do."

"Ain't got any. Come back when you can pay a copper. Then I'll be glad to sell you a loaf of bread," and he slammed the door.

Jack turned away and kicked at a cat in the alley. The thing hissed at him and jumped to the top of a rain barrel. Jack had a mind to grab it, lift the lid, and give the ugly creature a good dunking. But he knew his problems weren't the cat's fault. Instead, he hissed back at it until the cat scampered up on a shed roof out of his reach.

Jack was so discouraged when he came out of the alley that he was tempted to return to the river and tell Amy it was no use. But just then his ears caught the deep thump, thump, thump he'd heard the other morning on the cathedral steps. It had to be the Salvation Army band, but where was it?

He turned right and ran down the street, but the sound didn't get louder. Between the close buildings, the sound echoed so much that it was hard to tell from which way it came. Jack decided that it must be on the next street. He turned the corner and ran up to the next street. The band wasn't there, but the sound was louder. Now he could hear the flute and the horns. It sounded as good as a circus. He ran faster, and when he came around the next corner he was rewarded. There, halfway down the street was the Salvation Army band playing a song so joyful that it made Jack want to dance.

The band was on a loading platform for a warehouse. The platform was about the height of Jack's head. This put them up so everyone could see and hear them. But getting close was a different matter. The narrow street was jammed with people. Some were singing, some just standing there. Some were yelling, but Jack couldn't make out what they were saying.

He worked his way through the crowd until he was directly across the street from the band. Behind him was the open door to a pub. From there he could see the band clearly. Unfortunately, the general and the lady he had seen on the cathedral steps weren't among them. But he decided to listen to the singing and the band. Maybe afterwards he could ask them where Catherine Booth was. The song boomed out:

We're bound for the land
of the pure and the holy.
The home of the happy, the Kingdom of love;
Ye wanderers from God
in the broad road of folly,
O say, will you go to the Eden above?

Jack wasn't sure what it all meant, but he liked the tune, and he sure would like to go to some land where there weren't so many troubles. The chorus asked, "Will you go? Will you go?" over and over again with such earnestness that Jack almost shouted, "Yes."

Just then something went flying through the air and landed right in the bell of one of the horns. It jammed the horn into the player's mouth so hard that his lips began to bleed. Jack could see that the thing thrown was a dead cat.

A tremendous roar went up from the crowd. Some were cheering. Some were yelling to leave the band alone. "They're doing no harm."

More things went flying through the air: rocks, bottles, and mud that splattered on the band players turning their uniforms into an ugly mess.

The throwing seemed to be coming from a group of boys just about Jack's age, and most of them were right around him. As the fray continued, one after another yelled, "There, I got a hit!" "Count one for me." "Bull's-eye; that's a halfpenny for me."

The riot calmed down when the Salvation Army people got down from the loading platform.

"Hey, boy. Come here."

Jack looked around and through the doorway into the dark interior of a pub. A man stood there behind the bar wiping the counter, a pint of beer in his hand. His hair was cut short, but he had a huge walrus mustache, the ends of which drooped nearly to the bottom of his strong, square jaw. "Yeah, you," the man said nodding to Jack.

Jack stepped through the open door. It was an ordinary enough pub with a bar down one side and a big barrel on the end of the bar. It would hold beer. On the wall be-

hind were several smaller barrels on their sides with taps in the ends. They would hold whiskey, rum, and gin of the cheaper variety. Above them were bottles of the expensive stuff. Around the dark room were a few tables with chairs and a big old stove with a bucket full of coal beside it.

Jack approached slowly. The man just stood there, sipping from time to time from the pint in his hand. He wore the faded-red top of long-handled underwear frayed at the sleeves and around the neck. His black working pants were held up with wide braces, and his heavy boots were worn and scuffed. "You seen them Salvationists before?" he asked, pointing out the door.

"Yes, sir. I seen 'em once before," answered Jack.

"You live around here?"

"Sorta." Jack squirmed.

"Well, listen here. That Salvation Army intends to ruin my business. They want to shut down every gin house in London, and quite a few of my regulars have already converted. It's hittin' me where it hurts. You know what I mean? Right in my money pouch. But I'm a fair business man, and I'm willin' to pay for what I need. You seen them boys out there?"

"Yes, sir," Jack said, not exactly sure who the man meant but certain he'd find out soon enough.

"I pay each and every one of those boys a half-penny every time they make a hit that counts. You know what I mean?"

Jack shook his head no. He actually did have an idea what the man was saying, but he could hardly believe his ears.

"What I'm sayin' is, when they throw somethin' and they make a good hit, I keep score and pay a halfpenny each hit. The way I figure it, pretty soon those Salvationists will give up and find better things to do than trouble a legitimate business man. I got a legal license to run this pub, you know."

"Yes, sir," Jack said, not quite sure what he was agreeing with but feeling he ought to say something.

"So, what do you say? I'll pay you the same?"

"I got no cause to bother those people," Jack protested.

"No cause," the man growled through clenched teeth. "I just told you the cause, you little brat." And he made as if to lunge after Jack.

Jack turned to run out the door when the man changed the tone of his voice. "Wait. I didn't mean nothin' against you, boy. Look here. Come on back in here. You look like you could use a job. Am I right?"

"Yes, sir," said Jack. "Me and Amy, well, we need some . . ." Jack stopped, thinking it best to keep his troubles private.

"Okay, then. You need some money; I got a job for you to do. That's cause enough, wouldn't you say?"

Jack thought about it a moment. The hunger pains in his stomach were getting unbearable, and he'd promised to bring Amy something to eat. He could find that Mrs. Booth tomorrow. If they didn't get something to eat soon, neither of them would be strong enough to search the city for their uncle.

"All right. How do I get paid?"

"I'll be watching. You come back here after it's all over."

When Jack left the pub he expected that the Salvation Army would have packed up and left for some place safer. But instead one of the men was standing up on the platform speaking:

> A lot of you don't have jobs, some of you lack a place to live, and maybe you are even hungry. When Jesus saw people just like you, He cared. He cared enough to do something. There were five thousand men plus women and children in that crowd. That's a lot more than there are of you gathered here today on East Tenter Street.
>
> But Jesus asked a small boy to share what he had, and Jesus multiplied it. The Bible says that He "took the five loaves, and the two fishes, and looking up to heaven, he blessed, and brake, and gave the loaves to his disciples, and the disciples to the multitude. And they did all eat, and were filled: and they took up of the fragments that remained twelve baskets full."
>
> Jesus said, "Come unto me, all ye that labour and are heavy laden, and I will give you rest." But so many of you try to find your rest in gin and beer. You think you can drink your

troubles away, but the Bible says, "There is a way which seemeth right unto a man, but the end thereof are the ways of death."

Just then a howl went up from several people in the crowd, and a very ripe tomato landed right at the feet of the speaker splattering red juice all over his legs. Another tomato just missed the flag that flew above them.

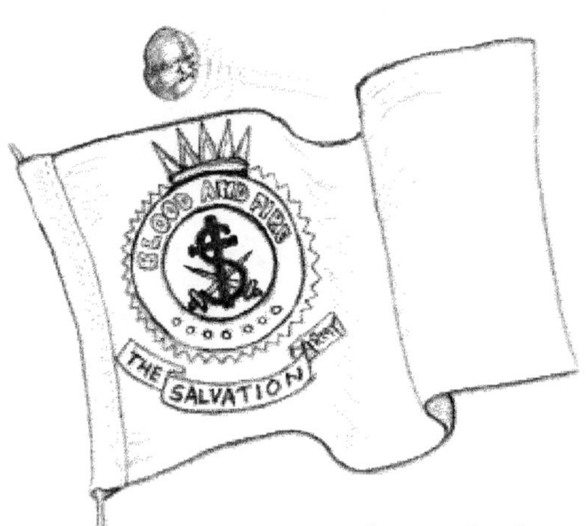

"Down with the Salvationists," yelled someone. "They just want to shut down our pubs." And several more things flew through the air.

Jack looked around and saw that some of the boys he had noticed before were again throwing things, so he, too, reached down and picked up a small pebble and gave it a gentle toss toward the speaker. He really didn't want to hurt anyone. The pebble flew through the air in a high arch and bounced harmlessly off the speaker's cap.

Jack glanced toward the pub. The owner was leaning casually in his doorway, his muscled arms crossed on his chest. He looked at Jack, scowled, and shook his head. Jack got the message: no halfpennies for little pebbles, even if he did score a bull's-eye. With a raised eyebrow the pub owner pointed to the street not far from Jack's feet. His hand barely moved as his finger made a sharp jab toward the spot on the ground and then another jab toward the speaker. Then the man looked away, ignoring Jack.

Jack looked down. There was a pile of fresh horse droppings. The man wanted him to throw those round, green "balls." Jack hesitated to pick them up. How could he? On the other hand, they wouldn't hurt anyone, and he was so hungry.

Tentatively Jack picked one up and gave it a toss. It went wide of its mark. Jack looked over to the pub owner. He shrugged slightly and looked away. Just then someone else's old shoe hit the speaker as he was repeating the verse about there being a way that seems right but leads to death. The crowd roared. Earlier—during the music—many people had seemed with the Salvation Army, even singing along. Now they had turned against them. They had become an ugly mob, enjoying being mean to the speaker.

Jack reached down and got another handful. This time he let fly. His aim was true, and the pub owner gave a slight nod. Jack threw again and again. Each time it was easier, almost like sport. He cheered when he got a second good hit and then a third.

Suddenly whistles began blowing and several police came down the street yelling, "Break it up!

Break it up! That's enough now. Everyone go on home."

Jack ducked back into the pub. The owner was already behind the bar wiping glasses as though nothing had happened. When he saw Jack, he said, "Get out of here. I don't want those cops finding one of you boys in here."

"But my money," protested Jack. "You saw me get three good hits. You owe me a penny and a half."

The man flipped Jack the money, and then snarled, "Now beat it."

Chapter 7

Bread and Water

JACK RAN BACK TO THE RIVER with a loaf of bread under one arm and a half-penny still in his pocket. He hadn't found Mrs. Booth, but he was able to keep his promise to get something for Amy and him to eat.

He'd gone back to the same bakery where the man had turned him away when he'd asked for a job. At first he thought that he'd never give that man his business. But the more he thought about it, it made him feel good to imagine slapping down his penny on the counter and demanding the biggest loaf of that good-looking white bread that he could see. He'd show that bakerman that he wasn't a beggar.

But when he got to the bakery, the man wasn't anywhere around. There was only a girl just a little older than Amy minding the shop. He bought the loaf and soon forgot about the ornery baker as he ran to the river.

He scrambled over the wall and dropped to the narrow strip of sand below. "Amy, Amy. Look here," he called as he worked his way over the rocks and around the pillar.

"Jack," Amy said as she got up from the sand and came toward him. "Where have you been? You've been away 'most all day. What you been up to?" Then she saw the loaf he was holding out. "Jack, where did you get that bread? You didn't steal it, did you?"

"No. I didn't steal it, and I didn't beg for it either. I earned some money, and I *bought* it. What's more, I still got a half-penny left, right here in my pocket." Jack pulled out the little copper and held it in the palm of his hand for Amy to inspect.

"Oh, Jack. I'm so hungry. I'm glad you got something to eat." She broke off a hunk of bread and began eating it. Jack grinned and did the same.

Then Jack realized that in spite of how hungry he had been, he had come all the way back home to share the bread with Amy before taking any himself. *It wouldn't have been right to eat it by myself,* he thought. *Whatever we've got is for sharing.* What was even stranger, he was thinking of this damp cave as "home." He looked around as he chewed. The place really was terrible.

"Did you find Mrs. Booth, Jack?"

"No. But I'll look some more tomorrow. She's bound to turn up soon." He didn't want to tell Amy that even though he hadn't found Catherine Booth, he had found the Salvation Army. Then she'd want to know why he hadn't asked the Army where Mrs. Booth was. That might lead to telling her how he'd earned the money, and he knew she'd be angry. But she sure was enjoying the bread, and so was he.

"Look, Jack," Amy said after taking a few bites, "I appreciate the bread, but finding Mrs. Booth is more important than wasting time earning money."

"Well, I tried to find her."

"Trying's not good enough. We've *got* to find her."

"Well, we gotta eat, too, don't we?" Jack said angrily.

"But we can't keep staying in this old cave. We *have* to find Uncle Sedgwick. And Mrs. Booth is our only hope."

Amy fell silent, and Jack didn't try to answer her. What could he say without giving himself away? Besides, when Amy got silent like that, Jack knew she was angry. He decided to be silent, too, hoping that pretty soon the whole thing would blow over. Jack knew it wasn't the best way to work out problems, but he was a little bit mad at himself, and he didn't want to admit to what he had done.

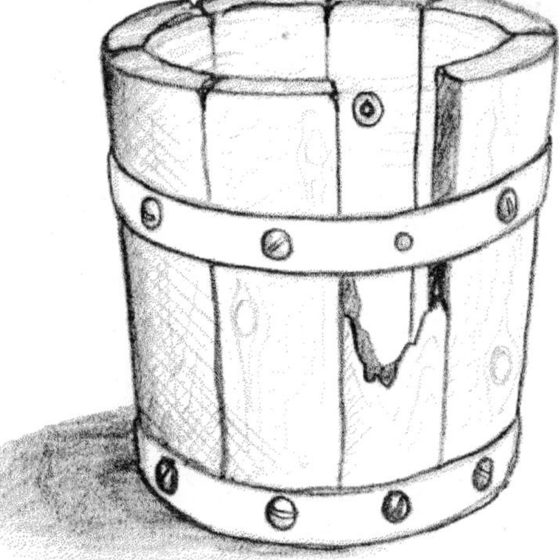

Sure enough, in a few moments Amy grabbed the old bucket and said, "I've been working on this broken bucket. I got the slats fitted back together, and I scrubbed it out with sand. Then all day I've been soaking it so the wood will swell. I put some rocks in it and held it under water. Now it doesn't leak. At least it holds water all the way up to where this one slat is broken. You could take it up and get some fresh water from the fountain up the street. Then we'd have drinking water."

"That'd be awful heavy to carry," said Jack looking at the bucket. It wasn't such a big bucket, but it didn't have a handle. And with the broken slat, he'd have to carry it tipped part way over to carry enough water to make it worth his trip. That could be heavy and hard to carry.

"But Jack, I haven't had anything to drink since we came down here last night. I was afraid to drink the river water. It's so dirty, I'm sure it would give a person the fever."

Her idea made sense, but he answered, "Let me just sit here and rest awhile. I been running all over town."

"Jack, I really am very thirsty."

"All right, all right. Just let me finish my piece of bread."

When Jack finally got back with the water, Amy had another fire laid. It was getting near dusk, and the lamplighter would be along soon. "I found a couple more sticks to use as matches," she said. "You know, if you were up there when the lamplighter came along, he'd probably just give you a light."

He probably would, but Jack didn't want to ask him. It would look so dumb asking for a light. Why would a boy on the street need to light a little stick? What would he tell the man, Jack wondered. "I'll just climb up the pole after he's gone," said Jack irritably. "Besides, since I fetched this water, I need a drink."

He started to reach his hands into their water bucket to scoop up a drink when Amy shouted, "Don't put your dirty hands in our drinking water. Go wash 'em first."

"I thought you said the river was dirty."

"So it is, too dirty to drink. But it's cleaner than your hands. It looks like you been playing in mud pies. And they stink too. What'd you do today to earn that money?"

"All right, give me that stick," Jack said, not wanting to answer Amy about his earnings. "I'll go up and get the stupid light, and wash my hands when I get back."

When the fire was blazing and the children were sitting around it eating some more bread, Amy bent her hurt foot back and forth testing her ankle. "It's a bit better, but I still don't think I should walk around town tomorrow. Would you mind going out by yourself again, Jack, to look for Mrs. Booth? We've got to find her! She's our only hope. We can't stay down here much longer."

Jack grunted but didn't feel like talking. What if he found Mrs. Booth and one of the Salvationists recognized him and told her he was one of the boys throwing things at the band? Maybe he'd just go looking for Uncle Sedgwick himself.

Later, when Amy was curled up sleeping by the fire with her green shawl thrown over her, he sat staring into the little flames. The song that the Salvationists were singing kept playing in his mind: “We’re bound for the land of the pure and the holy,” and then that haunting chorus: “Will you go? Will you go?”

The music had sounded pretty . . . he especially liked that horn. Thinking about it now made him feel bad that he had thrown stuff at them. Back and forth he argued with himself:

It wasn't that bad. I didn't really hurt anyone.

But, I must admit, they didn't do nothin' to deserve it. And even if they had, throwing horse manure is pretty mean.

But we needed the money.

Finally he drifted off into a fitful sleep filled with dreams of the Salvationists climbing on a train and singing. But every time Jack tried to get on the train with them, they would sadly shake their heads and say, "Sorry, we're bound for the land of the pure and the holy, and pure and holy you're certainly not."

Chapter 8

Rockets Away

THE NEXT MORNING Jack split the remaining bread with Amy and climbed up to the street. It was later than he'd started out the day before, and the morning was already sunny and warm. The air had the memory of summer to it, maybe one last time before the chill of autumn.

At home he had liked the autumn. The trees turned such beautiful colors, and the apples got shiny and juicy. Mama sure could make the best apple pies. But in the city there were no trees to fill one's eye with flaming reds and yellows. In the city it was just gray and chilly, not the kind of crispness that made you want to take a deep breath and run and play. Autumn in the city just reminded him that he had no mother to bake apple pies, and he had no home to keep warm in during the cold wet winter. And winter was surely coming.

But today *was* sunny, and Jack felt better than he had last night. Maybe those Salvationists wouldn't recognize him. Maybe finding Mrs. Booth was the best way to find Uncle Sedgwick. That was what Amy expected him to do; his sister had made it very clear. "It's the most important thing," she'd said. "We can't stay down here in this cave." When Jack pointed out that he had brought her some bread, she'd said, "What's a hunk of bread, Jack? We don't have a home, and winter's coming. You've got to find Mrs. Booth. Don't be doin' anything else today." Now as Jack trudged along, he knew Amy was right, but he was feeling pretty hungry again.

But where should he look? Finally he ended up on the street with the pub where the man had paid him the day before. Maybe the owner would know where the Salvationists were, and . . . maybe he could use some more "help." Just once more; then he could get something to eat. *Then* he would talk to Mrs. Booth.

When he got there and peeked through the door, the owner said, "You, boy, come in here. Don't stand there in the doorway. I don't want people seeing you hangin' 'round here."

As Jack walked up to the bar, he noticed three little stools on the floor in front of it. "What are these stools for?" he asked.

"Them's for children, of course. Where you from, anyway? You ain't from around here, or you'd for sure know what a children's stool was. Beside, you got a country accent to your talk."

"So what if I ain't from around here? Why do children need stools in here?" Jack insisted.

"It's so the little ones can reach the bar so's they can get themselves something to drink. What else?"

"You mean you serve beer to little children?"

"Ha! Only if they can't afford something stronger. It's good for business to get your customers started young. They develop a bigger thirst that way." The man polished the bar with his dirty apron for a few moments then said, "So what you want? You thirsty or something?"

"No," Jack said. "I was just wonderin' if . . . well, if you needed any more help with those Salvationists."

"Ah. So you want to earn some more money, do you?"

Jack nodded.

"Well, you go over on Queen Victoria Street, 'bout five streets down. Can't miss it—big building with a sign calling it 'The Christian Mission.' You hang 'round there, but not too close, mind you. You'll see some of the other boys about. Sooner or later a bunch of them Salvationists will come marching out. You follow them at a distance until they set up for their show. Then let 'em have it. You got it? You were a pretty good shot yesterday. Just keep it up."

"But how will you know how many hits I get so's to pay me?"

"I got someone watchin'—name's Jed. He'll keep track and report to me. You come by later and I'll pay you. But don't you come straight back here. I don't want no trouble. Understand?"

Jack headed toward Queen Victoria Street, but it was well into the afternoon before he found the building. As he approached, he debated with himself whether to try and earn some more money or go up to the door and see if Mrs. Booth was there. Maybe, he thought, *they've already gone.*

But the question was decided for him when one of the other boys noticed him looking at the place and called him to come around the corner. "What you doin' getting so close, mate?"

"I thought they might've gone out already," said Jack.

"Not yet, but you're going to give us all away, dummy," hissed the boy. "If they

know we're waitin' for them, they might not come out at all."

"Forget him," said an older boy standing near. "He don't know nothin'. I'm Jed, Winslow's man. You heard of me, boy?"

Jack nodded.

Jed snorted. "Those Salvationists go out every day, rain or shine, whether we throw stuff at them or not. They believe it's their God-given duty to save the world."

"Save the world?" asked Jack. "But I thought they were just trying to ruin people's business."

"Oh, yeah. They got it in for people in the sin business," Jed smirked.

"What's a sin business?" asked Jack.

"Gin houses, white slavers, and the like," said Jed. "Tell ya the truth, I'd just as soon they shut down the gin houses. My old man's a drunk, and he beats me every night he comes home drunk, which is nearly every night. So I say good riddance."

"Then how come you workin' for Winslow?" piped up one of the younger boys.

"It's a way to get a few coins," Jed shrugged.

Jack persisted. "But what are white slavers?"

"Don't you know what white slavers are?" The younger boy leaned close to Jack's ear. "They steal young girls."

"Yeah," said Jed, "*kidnap's* the word for it. Sometimes they even sell the girls to rich men over in France or Holland or Germany who want to buy a mistress."

A kind of dread made Jack's stomach tighten. "Isn't there some kind of a law against kidnapping girls? And how do they get them over to Europe anyway. Somebody would see 'em."

"Law? There ain't no law that sticks. That's one of the things the Salvation Army is always yellin' about—tryin' to get the government to stop the slavin'. As for gettin' the girls over to Europe, that's easy." Jed was clearly enjoying his role of dispensing worldly wisdom. He lowered his voice. "They drug 'em. When the girls are unconscious they nail 'em in coffins with air holes drilled in 'em and ship 'em over. Ain't nobody ever asks to see a dead body inside a coffin, so no one ever knows that it's a live girl inside. 'Cept . . . they ain't always alive."

The knot in Jack's stomach got tighter. "What do you mean?" he demanded.

"Sometimes they drug the girls too much and they die," Jed said matter-of-factly. "And *sometimes* they don't give 'em enough, and they wake up 'fore they get there." He paused for effect. "What would *you* do if you woke up and found yourself nailed inside a dark coffin? Why, some of them girls go screamin' crazy, and some just plain die trying to scratch their way out."

All the boys were silent as they considered such a horrible fate. Finally one of the younger boys said, "My cousin was kidnapped by a white slaver, and ain't no one ever heard from her since."

"Your cousin?" asked Jack. "How old was your cousin?"

"Thirteen, but she looked older."

"Thirteen, fourteen, it don't make no difference," snorted Jed. "Those slavers will take any girl about that age."

Just then they heard a familiar boom, boom, boom. The Salvation Army band was coming out.

The boys stayed hidden until the band went marching down the street, then they followed just out of sight. Along the way they gathered things to throw. Jed picked up some stinking old bones that the dogs hadn't eaten. The other boys found some rotten tomatoes in a pile of garbage, which they loaded into a rag, gathering up the four corners to make a bag in which to carry them.

Jack looked but didn't see Mrs. Booth with the band. Good. After he got his money from Winslow, he could go back to The Christian Mission and ask for Mrs. Booth. But Jack was thinking hard. If the Salvation Army was against those white slavers, wasn't it better to help them instead of fight them? But his growling stomach kept him following the band with the other boys.

This time the Army went down near the docks where the ships loaded and unloaded. The docks were wide and stuck out into the water like big fingers. Warehouses were built on some of the docks. Others were just flat platforms to receive goods from the ships that would tie up between them.

The boys stayed back while the Salvationists set up right at the beginning of one dock, with their backs to its warehouse. There was no ship tied up at that dock. The next dock was the flat type. On the other side of it was a huge, square-rigged merchant ship. Dozens of sailors and dock workers were preparing it to set sail. It was to these men—across the narrow slip of water between the docks—that the Salvationists planned to sing and preach. Of course, there were plenty of people going back and forth along the street at the foot of the docks who would hear them too. And that's where the boys stood behind several bales of cotton waiting for their chance to pelt the Salvationists.

When the group was ready, one of the Salvationists picked up a megaphone to speak. It was General Booth himself. Somehow, as the boys had followed along, Jack hadn't seen Booth in the group. But there he was. Quickly Jack looked to see if Mrs. Booth was also there, but he didn't see her. Then the general began speaking.

> Many people wonder why we call ourselves the Salvation Army. We're an army because we fight. We fight for the souls of men and women and boys and girls. We fight to release them from the shackles of sin and bring them to Jesus. We fight to bring them to that land of the pure and the holy.
>
> Listen to me all you brothers who sail the seven seas and work these docks. While women weep, as they do now, I'll fight; while little children go hungry, I'll fight; while men go to prison, in and out, in and out, as they do now—yes, I can see some of you know what I'm talking about—well, I'll fight. While there is a drunkard left, while there is a poor lost girl upon the streets, where there remains one dark soul without the light of God—I'll fight! I'll fight to the very end!

That's why we're called the Salvation Army. But before I tell you about Jesus Christ and how He can free you from sin, listen to this beautiful song, sung by our three Hallelujah Lasses and accompanied by Charlie Fry and his Hallelujah Band.

As the band was getting tuned up, Jack's attention was distracted by a couple of sailors on the dock across from the Salvationists. One was holding a small torch as the other tipped over a crate and then wrestled it around. The first one bent down and was doing something with the torch. Then he stood up, threw the torch into the water, and both men started running. It was then that Jack recognized one of the sailors as the "river rat" he'd almost hit in the boat on the river the morning before.

Suddenly from the crate on the dock there came a cloud of white smoke and a loud "hissst" as something rocketed out of the crate, across the water, and landed among the Salvationists. Before the Salvation Army people could jump back, several more rockets flew into their midst. They were signal flares, shooting right at the Hallelujah Lasses. As Jack watched, two of the women were hit directly by the flaming torpedoes while other Salvationists jumped around dodging the flares as they landed among them. Soon there was thick smoke everywhere. The last thing Jack saw was the two women who had been hit trying to put out their flaming clothes.

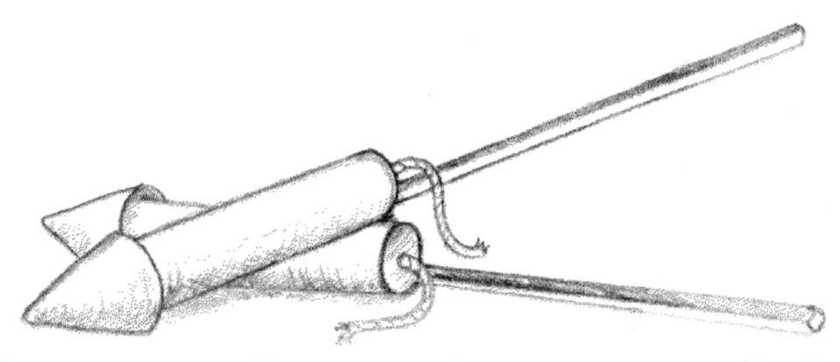

Everyone on the street began to run. Jack and the other boys were running with them. People scattered in every direction, and Jack found himself alone. When he had no more breath to run further, he slowed to a walk. He was heading back toward the river cave. Why would those sailors do such a thing? Yesterday Jack and the other boys had been throwing trash. It made a mess and might have left a few bruises, but those flares could have killed people. What was going on?

As Jack climbed over the rail beside the river, he felt dejected. The afternoon would soon be over and he still had not contacted Mrs. Booth. And today he had no money and couldn't bring back anything for Amy to eat. As he thought about it, Jack dreaded facing her. How could he tell her about what had happened?

He didn't call out to her when he climbed around the pillar, but even if he had, it would have done no good. She wasn't there. All that was left in the cave was her green shawl and a strange deep gouge in the sand by the river.

Chapter 9

Kidnapped

"Amy! Amy!" Jack called. She must be nearby somewhere. But there was no answer. He kicked around amongst the trash at the back of the cave. He didn't know what he was looking for . . . maybe she'd left a note.

Nothing.

Jack picked up Amy's shawl. What now? Maybe she'd gotten tired of staying in the cave and had climbed up to the street to walk around. Should he look for her or just wait? As he stood uncertainly at the cave opening, his eyes were drawn again to the deep gouge in the sand at the river's edge. He inspected it more carefully. It was about four feet long, coming right out of the river. In fact, at the water's edge, where the water was no more than an inch deep, Jack could see that the groove extended into the river. Something had been dragged up out of the river, something heavy like a boat.

Of course! That was it. Someone had beached a boat in the cave. As he looked more closely, Jack could see large boot prints in the sand. Then, right next to the water, where the sand was damp and firm, Jack saw Amy's footprint on top of one of the boot prints.

The clues were clear: A boat had stopped, and Amy had gone away in it. But who could have been in the boat, and where could Amy have gone? Jack looked out over the river in the late afternoon sun. There were several boats on the river, but none small enough to be beached in the cave.

"Amy! Amy!" Jack yelled with all his might out over the water. His voice echoed in the hollow confines of the cave and off the stone bridge above. But there was no answer from his sister.

"Amy, Amy, Amy," muttered Jack as he stumbled around inside the cave, kicking the sand with his feet. "Don't leave me, Amy. Papa's dead, and Mama's gone . . ." He still didn't like saying the words out loud that admitted his mother was dead. Jack kicked angrily at the charred sticks in the fire pit. "And now you've run off! How will we ever find Uncle Sedgwick?"

That's when Jack noticed the water bucket. It had been tipped over. He felt the sand around it. Wet. *Strange*, thought Jack. *Amy wouldn't dump out our water.* But someone had, and not very long ago, either, because the sand was more than damp. It was wet, very wet, like someone had just poured out the water ten or fifteen minutes ago. One of Amy's footprints was planted squarely in this wet sand too. But it was also pulled off to the side as though her foot had been dragged away.

A terrible realization began to sweep over Jack. Amy hadn't gone off on some errand, and she hadn't gone off willingly with someone in a boat. She had fought. She had struggled, and then she had been taken away against her will.

Amy had been kidnapped.

That's why the water bucket was tipped over; that's why her shawl had been left behind, and that's what all the tracks in the sand indicated. Someone had grabbed her and pulled her into that boat. She had been kidnapped. There was no getting around it.

As soon as Jack realized what had happened, he felt certain he knew who had done it. It had to be those two men who had fired the flares at the Salvationists, the ones Jack almost hit when he was throwing rocks at the river rat. Yeah, those river rats were the only people who knew anyone was staying in this cave. And they would have had time. If they had come on the river instead of running all around through the streets of London as Jack had done, they could easily have been here and gone before Jack arrived. But why? Why would they have wanted to kidnap Amy?

Somewhere in the back of Jack's mind there was a clue. They had been angry at Jack for throwing rocks and had threatened him if he ever did it again. But there was something else, something they had said—not to him, but—about . . . about what? And then Jack remembered. It was what they'd said about Amy. The one rowing had said something like, "Hey, Rodney, it's a girl." And the other one, the big burly one who had been standing up yelling at Jack, had said, “Yeah, and just about the right age too.”

“The right age for what?” wondered Jack aloud, and the moment he said it a cold chill ran down his spine. Those men where white slavers. And they’d taken Amy.

Jack fought back the wave of panic that swept over him. He had to find his sister. He had to get her back.

Out of the cave Jack ran, almost slipping on the rocks as he scrambled around the pillar. In a moment he had scampered up the wall and was on the street. Where would he go? Whom could he ask? How could he find her? He ran along the river’s edge looking at all the boats going peacefully back and forth below. Amy had to be in one of them. But what if he were going the wrong direction? While he ran himself breathless going up the river, what if the kidnappers were rowing as fast as they could down the river with Amy tied up under an old blanket in the bottom of the boat so no one could see her? Jack’s mind ran wild as he tried to imagine what could be happening to her. Would she be nailed in a coffin and thrown down into the dark, damp hold of a ship? Would she die from too much of the drug? Or would she wake up and go crazy trying to scratch her way out? Would she be sold to someone who would beat her? And then he sucked in his breath with a start—whether the person who bought her beat her or not, she wouldn’t be free. He might not ever see her again.

Jack ran all the faster. He dodged through day merchants pushing their carts back from the market. He pushed aside groups of other children in his way. He tripped over the bucket of a fisherman who stood with a pole and line at the wall by the river's edge.

But he never saw Amy. In fact, he didn't see even one boat that looked like the one the sailors had been in.

Finally, Jack fell to the cobblestone street exhausted and crying in great sobs as he tried to catch his breath. It was useless. He could never find his sister this way. He could run up and down the Thames River and all over London for days without ever seeing her. By then she might be shipped off to face some horrible life. . . . He didn't want to think about it.

Slowly he picked himself up and walked back toward the cave. Maybe he was wrong. Maybe he was imagining all this. Yeah, that had to be it. Amy wasn't really kidnapped. She had just gone out to get some fresh air and would be back in their cave by the time he got there. He should just settle down and quit imagining the worst.

He took a deep breath and thought about the Salvationists. If there was a God like they said there was, He certainly wouldn't let such a terrible thing happen to his sister. After all, she had never done anything so bad. She hadn't even thrown stuff at the Salvationists.

And then another thought crossed Jack's mind. What if God was punishing her because of the bad things he had done? "Oh, God," he found himself saying, "please don't. Don't let her be kidnapped. I won't throw any more stuff at that Salvation Army, and I won't steal any more apples or anything."

But when he got to the cave, it was just as he had left it. Amy was not there.

Chapter 10

The Devil's Mile

When Jack got back up to the street, the lamplighter was coming along, but Jack didn't care. Unless he could find Amy, he wouldn't need a fire tonight.

What was he going to do? Somehow he had to get help. He thought of trying to find a bobby, but then he remembered what Jed had said: there were no laws the policemen could enforce to stop the slave trade. The Salvation Army was fighting to get such laws passed, but so far there was very little the police could do. Besides, why would a bobby believe a wild story like his?

No, the police weren't likely to search the city for his sister on the mere word of a boy, who had no home and no parents to back up his story. But if he could just find out where they were holding Amy . . . then maybe someone would believe him and help.

Slowly an idea began to form in Jack's mind. Maybe Winslow, the pub owner, would know about the slave trade. At least he was dead set against the Salvation Army and their attempts to change things, and he wasn't against doing some shady deals on the side.

It wasn't much of an idea, but it was the only one he had. Jack set off through the darkening streets at a jog.

When Jack got to the pub, Winslow was busy with customers. In fact, the popular bar was full of loud-talking workmen who probably should have been home with their families. A woman played a piano as several men around her sang songs. The bright flames in the fireplace reflected off the bright copper pots hanging from pegs on the wall. Candles sat in the windows and elsewhere to light the room.

Jack stepped up to the bar and tried to get Winslow's attention. When the pub owner saw Jack, he scowled and kept on filling pints with beer. When he finally came Jack's way, he was obviously irritated. "Whatcha want? Don't go tellin' me I owe ya some ha'pennies. I heard what happened down at the dock today, and I don't pay boys who run off."

"I didn't come to collect," Jack said anxiously. "I just wanna ask if you know a big sailor named Rodney?"

"Maybe I do, and maybe I don't. Rodney's a mighty common name. What's it to you?"

"He kidnapped my sister, and I got to find her," Jack pleaded.

Winslow's scowl deepened. "Listen, boy. I don't have nothin' to do with kidnappin' girls. Never have, never will. I just run a legal pub."

"Yeah, but both you and Rodney don't like the Salvation Army."

"How do you know that?"

"'Cause it was Rodney and another guy with him that fired those flare rockets at the Salvation Army this afternoon. I saw 'em do it," said Jack.

"So what?" said Winslow. "Rodney's got his reasons for not liking the Army, and I got mine. That doesn't mean we work together."

"But you do know him, then?"

"I know who he is, nothin' more," said the pub owner as he walked back down the bar to serve a new customer.

When he returned, Jack persisted. "All I want to know is where he took my sister. Do you know where Rodney might be?"

"I don't know nothin'. Understand? I don't want anyone thinkin' that I'm tied in with Rodney and his kind. It's a dirty business they're into." Winslow turned away to draw a pint of beer for a customer. In a few minutes he came back over to Jack. "You say he took your sister? Hmmm. Come to think of it, I have seen Rodney hanging out with Mary Jaffries. She runs at least a dozen bawdyhouses. There's four of 'em over on Church Street in Chelsea, and another just over on Gray's Inn Road. But there's one I've heard tell where Rodney hangs out. Up on Devil's Mile. You might try there for your sister."

"Where's the Devil's Mile?" said Jack.

"Ain't the real name. That's just what they call it.

Uh . . . what's the name of that street? Hey, Peter," Winslow called to a customer across the room. "What's the name of that street they call the Devil's Mile?"

"You mean Islington?"

"Yeah, that's it, Islington High Street. But it ain't a mile long; it's just a little short street."

"But where is it?" asked Jack.

"Stubborn boy, ain't you! Drivin' me crazy." He stared at Jack for a few moments. Then he said, "All right. Here's what you do. Go up Aldersgate. It turns into Goswell. Soon's you cross Pentonville Road, you're right there. 'Bout a mile and a half from here. Can't miss it. Now beat it. Go on; get out of here."

Jack discovered that you *could* miss the street and rather easily, too, especially at night. But once he found it, he knew it was the "Devil's Mile." Every other door seemed to be a pub that was open and noisy, even this late in the evening. Many people were out on the street, some well-dressed and businesslike and others dirty and drunk. Jack even had to walk around three men sleeping on the sidewalk, or maybe they were passed out drunk.

But how was he going to find Amy? She wasn't likely to be in one of the pubs, or she could have just walked out. Winslow had mentioned a "house" operated by some woman. But how would he know which one? There were several houses along this street . . . at least between the pubs. Jack wandered along the street, looking in the door of every pub and studying every house hoping to find some clue.

Then from across the street Jack heard a familiar voice. A huge man came out of a pub and yelled back to someone inside: "You don't need to worry. I always deliver my merchandise." It was Rodney, and he was coming across the street right toward Jack! If Rodney hadn't seen him yet, he soon would. There was nowhere to hide. Suddenly a horse and carriage came clattering down the street at a fast trot. It was a fancy four-wheeler with two little lanterns twinkling brightly.

Yelling at the driver, Rodney jumped back out of the street to avoid being run over. The driver swerved toward Jack and tried to slow down as he cursed back at Rodney. "Look before you stagger across the street, you fat lout, or you'll end up greasing my wheels."

It was Jack's chance. As the carriage swung past, he jumped on the back step where a coachmen sometimes stood. He held on with all his might and crouched down in the shadows as the carriage whisked him down the street away from Rodney. When he looked back, Rodney had crossed the street and was entering the house right by where Jack had been standing.

That must be where he's hiding Amy, thought Jack.

He dropped off the carriage and ran back up the street, weaving between the night revelers and jumping over the drunks until he got to the house into which Rodney had disappeared.

But how could he find out whether his sister was inside? Lights glowed dimly in the windows behind heavy red drapes, and piano music tinkled softly through the night air. From time to time, Jack could hear laughter within the house.

Finally, Jack could wait no longer. He had to do something, so he dashed up the steps and pounded on the door. Immediately the door opened, and a pinched-faced little doorman leaned out. "What do you want?"

"I'm looking for my sister, Amy," Jack said. "Is she here?"

The man sneered. "I don't know you, so how could I know who your sister is. Now be gone with ya," and he started to close the door.

"Wait," said Jack. "Maybe you've seen her. She's a little taller than me, and she has dark red hair. It's curly, and she's very pretty. Have you seen her? She's been kidnapped by a man named Rodney. He just came in . . ."

At the mention of Rodney's name, the man slammed the door before Jack could say more.

Jack stood on the steps wondering what to do until he saw another horse-drawn cab approaching. The cab stopped, and a finely dressed man opened the door, stepped out and approached the house. Jack was feeling desperate. "Excuse me, sir," he said, "my sister has been kidnapped, and I think she's being held inside this house by some very bad people."

The man reacted as if he had seen a ghost. He stared wide-eyed at Jack for a moment then raised his cane in a threatening manner. “You haven’t seen me here,” he commanded. Then he turned and ran after the cab that was just starting to pull away. He caught the driver’s attention and got him to stop. Then the man rode off without looking back.

Jack realized that if he was going to free his sister he wasn’t likely to get any help from anyone on the street. He would have to find some other way to get Amy.

Most of the buildings and houses on Devil’s Mile were built side by side with no space between them. But three houses down, Jack found a little passage between two buildings that allowed him to walk back to the alley behind the house. The passageway was even too narrow to drive a cart through. Jack turned and walked up the alley, counting three houses to the building he thought Amy was in. Maybe, he thought, he could find a way inside through a back entrance.

The only light was from a half moon that shown through a hazy sky. Laundry hung like dancing ghosts from clotheslines strung across the alley. When Jack was sure he had located the correct building, he was disappointed to find the back door securely locked. The door actually led into a low lean-to shed that was built onto the back of the house. Above the shed were two windows leading directly into the house. They were both shuttered. But through the cracks in the shutters on one of the windows, Jack made out the dim shine of a light. *Could Amy be in there?* Jack wondered.

A little further down the alley, he found some old boxes. He brought them back to the shed and piled one on top of the other. Then he climbed up. It gave him just enough height that he was able to pull himself up onto the roof of the shed. From there he crept toward the window with the light. He tapped on the shutter softly, but there was no response. He tapped again harder and called out, "Amy! Amy! Are you in there?"

In the quiet evening, he was certain that everyone in the neighborhood could hear him. But still there was no answer.

Jack waited a moment adjusting his weight so as not to slip down the shed's roof. Finally, he decided he had to try for all he was worth. What difference would it make if he was careful not to get caught but never found Amy? So he beat on the shutter with his fists and yelled with all his might.

The shutters flung open, knocking him down the roof where he fell to the ground just as a man leaned out and bellowed, “What do you want out here, anyway? Get out of here or I’ll beat the daylights out of you!” Then the shutters closed.

Jack picked himself up and started to run when he heard another voice. It was a girl's voice coming from behind the dark window, the one with the shutters still locked. "Jack! Jack! Is that you?"

It was Amy!

"Amy!" Jack called back in relief. "I came to get you. Let's get out of here."

"I can't. I'm locked in this little room."

"Are you okay? Have they hurt you?"

"No. No one's hurt me yet." And then Jack could hear her start to cry. "But Jack," Amy sobbed, "you gotta get me out of here. I'm scared. This is an awful place, and I think they are going to take me away tomorrow."

Just then someone came running out of the little passage between the buildings and into the alley. In the dim light Jack could see that he was big, and he was headed right for Jack.

Chapter 11

Midnight Raid

JACK HAD ONLY A GLIMPSE of the man running down the alley toward him, but he was sure it was Rodney. He took off the other way not knowing if he could get out of the alley in that direction. He stumbled over trash and fell two or three times, but finally he came out into another street where the glow of a distant street lamp gave him some hope. He ran faster, and after he had crossed a couple other streets, he was convinced he was no longer being chased.

He slowed to a walk, keeping to the shadows where he couldn't be seen, but his heart went on racing for quite some time.

He had found Amy; that was good. But finding her confirmed all his worst fears. If he couldn't get her out of that place, she would soon be shipped away, and he might never see her again.

He had to get some help! But who could help him? Who would believe him? Who would even care? And what could one or even two people do. What he needed was an army to raid that place and rescue his sister . . . .

Jack stopped in his tracks. That was it—an army! What was it General Booth had said down by the docks? "While there is a poor lost girl upon the streets . . . I'll fight! I'll fight to the very end!" Jack needed the *Salvation Army*. Maybe they would help him save his sister.

It was nearly midnight when Jack found the Salvation Army headquarters again on Queen Victoria Street, not far from the river. Everything looked so different at night that he almost didn't recognize it. Inside all the lights were out. But Jack was determined. He pounded on the door until a young man in his nightshirt and looking very tired answered. A candle flickered weakly in the room behind him.

"I have to speak to General Booth," Jack said urgently.

"He's not available right now," the man said. "He's trying to sleep. Look, son. If you need something to eat, come back tomorrow morning. We'll serve you breakfast."

"That's not it! I have to talk to the general."

"I'm sorry. He can't be disturbed. He's very tired."

Jack was close to tears. "But he said he would fight! And I need him to fight for my sister right now. Tomorrow may be too late!"

The young man opened the door a little wider. "What do you mean, 'fight for your sister'?"

"She's been kidnapped," said Jack, fighting back the tears. "Rodney took her—that, that sailor down at the docks, the one who fired those flare rockets at you today! Now she's locked up in a house on the Devil's Mile. They're going to ship her out tomorrow!"

The young man reached out and pulled Jack through the doorway. "I see. That's different. Come on in, son." He led Jack through a long hall to a huge kitchen where he lit a lamp and put it on a small table. "Wait here," he said. "Oh, if you want something to eat, help yourself to those bran muffins on the counter."

Jack thought that muffins had never tasted so good. In his fear for Amy he had forgotten he hadn't eaten anything all day. He was licking his fingers when the general himself came into the kitchen, his steely gray hair sticking almost straight up and his shirt buttoned crooked.

"What's this about your sister being kidnapped?" he boomed. His eyes looked like a storm about to strike.

So Jack told him, and the general kept asking questions, his voice getting more gentle as he talked. Soon the whole story came out . . . including Jack throwing stuff at the Salvation Army to earn some money for bread and the fact that he and Amy had been living in a cave under a bridge since their mother died.

"This is terrible," thundered the general. He stalked back and forth in the kitchen tugging on his beard. Then he asked Jack to describe again very carefully where Amy was being held. When he had asked a few more questions about the shed on which Jack had climbed, the general mused, "Hmmm. If they haven't moved her to a different room, there's a chance we could climb up there with a bar and pry open those shutters. We just might be able to have her out of there before they even notice. But son, I need to know whether you are telling me the whole truth, and that you're not leaving anything out. Because if we make a mistake, we could be in very big trouble for breaking into some citizen's home. Now are you completely sure your sister is being held there against her will?"

"Yes, sir!" said Jack. "She talked to me through the shutters. She said, 'I got to get out of here,' and I know it was Amy."

"All right," said the general. "Philip," he turned to the young man in the nightshirt, "get a couple of the other officers, and let's go see what we can do."

When Jack and the four Salvation Army men got back to the Devil's Mile, a cab was just pulling away from the front of the house. “Is that the house?” asked General Booth in a low voice.

“That’s it,” said Jack. “And the way to get around back is through that little passage between those two buildings up there. Come on; I’ll show you.”

“Not yet,” said the general. “First we ask God’s help.”

They all stood in a little circle in the shadows across the street a little way down from their objective, and the general’s gentle voice spoke quietly. “Lord, You know of the great sins that plague this city and the terrible suffering it brings to so many people. Now we ask Your help and protection as we try to free one of your little ones. Give us success, and protect her from any harm. Amen.” The general straightened.

“All right, son. Lead the way.”

When Jack and the men got to the shed behind the house, the boxes he had piled up were still there. It gave him hope that Rodney and his gang had not done too much to secure Amy.

The boxes, however, weren’t strong enough to hold the bigger men, so they gave a boost to young Philip. From the top of the shed, Philip pulled one of the other men up.

“Now you listen to me, Jack,” whispered the general. “If we get your sister out, but someone discovers us in the process, grab her and take off running back to headquarters. We’ll try to delay them to give you some time. Think you can find headquarters again?”

"I think so," said Jack. He was trying not to shiver in the cold night air.

Just then Jack looked up to see the two Salvation Army officers getting ready to pry open the shutters over one of the windows with the iron bar they had brought with them. "No!" said Jack in a desperate whisper. "Not that window. The other one." He'd almost been too late.

The men moved like cats across the shed roof to the other window. In the near black night, they looked at Jack. "Yeah, that one," he whispered.

The men put their bar between the two shutters and gave a pull. There was a creak, but nothing happened. Again they pulled. This time there was a loud snap and a splintering sound as the shutters swung open. Both men hung on to the swinging shutters so as not to lose their balance on the steep roof.

From inside the room there came a scream.

"Amy!" Jack called. "Amy, open the window."

Amy's scream had come only from the fright of waking up in the middle of the night to see a couple dark shapes outside her window. Now Jack could just barely see Amy standing inside the window working frantically to get the window open. But just as the latch came free, and Amy was raising the window, a light appeared in the room behind her.

"Hey, what are you doing there?" came a woman's angry voice. "You get back in here. You can't leave."

Amy was climbing out the window just as the woman caught her and tried to drag her back inside.

"Help her!" screamed Jack to the two men on the shed roof.

They grabbed on to Amy's arms while the woman inside held fast to one of her legs, but it wasn't much of a tug-of-war. In just moments the men had pulled her free, and Amy was standing on the roof holding tightly to her rescuers.

The woman inside was screaming for help as the two men on the roof lowered Amy to the general and the other man in the alley below. As soon as Amy was safe on the ground, the general said to Jack,

"Don't wait for us. Get her out of here. We'll see you later."

Jack and Amy ran for all they were worth. They were three streets away before Jack even dared to look back. No one seemed to be following. "Let's slow down," he gasped. "We've got a long way to go." But Amy kept running, her arms swinging like windmills, and her hair flying back.

When Jack caught up to her side again, he noticed in the dim light of a street lamp that tears were streaming across her cheeks. "Amy, what's the matter? Come on; slow down." He reached out and put his hand on her shoulder. She jerked away, but she did slow down. As soon as she was walking, great sobs began to shake her body, and she buried her face in her hands.

"Hey, Amy, what's the matter? Are you hurt?" Jack awkwardly patted her shoulder, while he tried to catch his breath.

She shook her head wildly. "No," she sobbed. "I'm just so glad we're back together." She stopped and threw her arms around her brother. Jack looked around, but there was no one on the street to notice. He wrapped his arms around his sister and hugged her close. In a few moments they continued on toward the Salvation Army headquarters.

Within an hour, the strange little group was all together again, being served hot tea in headquarter's kitchen by none other than Mrs. Catherine Booth. As the men told their story with big gestures and Mrs. Booth murmured sympathetically, Jack and Amy looked at each other. Finally, they could ask the lady with the smiling eyes about their Uncle Sedgwick, the tailor.

Chapter 12

Escape to America

WHEN THE STORY was told and second cups of tea had been poured, Amy spoke up. "Mrs. Booth," she said, "one day when we were looking for our uncle, we asked another tailor about him. He said you did business with our uncle for a while. Do you remember him?"

Mrs. Booth knit her forehead.

"Well, it's been almost two years since I've used any tailor. We sew all our uniforms ourselves these days. It helps teach the new recruits a useful trade."

"But when you did use a tailor," said Jack, "you used to go to one over on . . . oh, I can't remember the name of the street. Anyway, he was an old man, and he said you had been his regular customer until you switched to our uncle, Sedgwick Masters. Don't you remember?"

"Why yes, Sedgwick Masters the tailor. Now I remember. I used him for only a few months. Actually, he was the one who suggested that we sew our own uniforms."

"But where is he now?" asked Amy. "You see, he's our only living relative. We don't have any other family. We've got to find him so we can have some place to live. Mother said he had some money, so he could take us in."

The lines on Mrs. Booth's forehead deepened. "I don't know where he is anymore. But I don't think he's in London. At least the other day I noticed that his old shop was empty. Come to think of it, he used to talk a lot about the great opportunities overseas—in India, Canada, even Australia. Maybe he finally packed up and left. I just don't know."

Both children sat in stunned silence. Their last hope for finding their uncle had evaporated. Amy blinked away the hot tears that sprang to her eyes. It was a terrible lost feeling not to have any home. The cave wasn't comfortable, but they'd made the best of it—even pretended it was an adventure—

because there had always been hope, the hope that they would soon find their uncle and have a home and family again. Now that hope was gone. She had been rescued, but now what were they going to do?

Jack looked down at the floor, hoping that the hair that fell over his eyes would hide the fact that he was crying. But looking down made him feel all the more hopeless. The sole of his right shoe was tearing loose from the uppers, and they had no money to buy new ones, or even to get it fixed. And they couldn't go back to the cave—it was too dangerous. What would they do?

Mrs. Booth stepped between the children and put a hand on each of their shoulders. "There, there," she said, "remember what our Lord Jesus said: 'Are not two sparrows sold for a farthing? and one of them shall not fall on the ground without your Father knowing.' So, 'Fear ye not therefore, ye are of more value than many sparrows.' God will not forget you, my young friends. Besides, for now you can stay here with us. And now it's very, very late. Let's get to bed."

The cots were plain, but they were the first warm beds that Jack and Amy had slept in for many nights. A feather bed in a palace couldn't have felt better.

Three days later the children were enjoying their life at the Salvation Army headquarters. They had received a bath, clean clothes, and were eating three good meals a day. Jack even had a different pair of shoes. They weren't new, but at least they weren't falling apart. The children had also been given chores to do, but Jack and Amy didn't mind; it made them feel useful. Philip Barker, the young man who had met Jack at the door the night he came for help, and his wife, Martha, had taken special responsibility for the children. They assigned chores for the children to do and found clothes for them.

One day the Barkers took Jack and Amy to Mrs. Witherspoon's. There they paid the debt for the rent that the children had been unable to pay when their mother had been so sick. "I ought to charge interest, it's gone unpaid for so long," grumbled Mrs. Witherspoon.

"Well, it's only been a few days. That hardly seems appropriate . . ." began Philip.

"We'd be glad to add whatever you think's fair," broke in Martha, "provided you tell us where their mother was buried. I'm sure the children would want to visit her grave. And, of course, you will be returning their trunk now, won't you?"

"You can have that old trunk, but you'll have to go up stairs and get it yourself. I'm not going to carry the thing down for you."

"And where was Mrs. Crumpton buried?"

"How should I know? I'm not the mortician."

"But you would have a receipt. It's the law," said Philip, holding a small coin out toward Mrs. Witherspoon.

"Oh, all right. It's probably around here somewhere."

The Barkers took the children that very afternoon to the cemetery and found the pauper's grave where their mother was registered as having been buried. They stood there a long time and cried as they thought about her and the ways their life had changed in the last few days.

That evening they cried again as they went through their belongings from the old trunk. Jack and Amy had never prayed much before, but every evening before bedtime, the Barkers asked them to come to their room for family prayers. There Philip read a few verses from the Bible, and both he and Martha prayed. This evening the prayers were for the children's loss of their mother and that God would comfort them. "Would either of you like to pray too?" Martha asked. Jack liked the way she smiled at them—but he wasn't sure about praying, not even at a time like this. But Amy prayed, and afterward, Jack wished he had too.

The Barkers prayed like Jesus was a friend sitting right there in the room with them. It made Jack feel like the Barkers really cared about them and that God cared about them too. It was almost like being part of the family.

But the children were afraid that this good arrangement couldn't last. And sure enough, one afternoon about a week later, General Booth called them into his office. When they entered the small room, the general was sitting behind his large desk and Catherine Booth was sitting in a large straight-backed chair to his side. Standing with their backs to the tall bookcase were also Philip and Martha Barker.

Oh no. This is it, thought Jack. *They're going to tell us we have to go. Or maybe the general remembers what I told him about throwing stuff at the Salvation Army, and he's going to punish us.*

After the general cleared his throat, he spoke as though he were addressing a crowd of people on the streets. "Miss Amy Crumpton and Master Jack Crumpton," he began, "you may not realize it, but Officers Philip and Martha Barker, here, have been commissioned for a very important mission.

"You see, a year and a half ago we dispatched Commissioner George Scott Railton and seven hallelujah lasses to establish a beachhead for the Gospel of our Lord Jesus Christ in New York City in the United States of America. They have been very successful in the fight and are now asking for reinforcements. The Barkers have volunteered as brave soldiers of the Cross, along with another family. Soon they will be leaving and will no longer be able to care for you here."

Just as I thought, worried Jack. *It's all over.*

"However," continued the general, "we'd like to give you a choice. If you choose, you can stay here working in the headquarters, doing the kinds of jobs you have been doing for the last few days. Maybe in time you'll be able to track down your uncle, but I can't make any promises in that regard. Actually, Philip has been doing some investigation around town, and there doesn't seem to be a trace of Sedgwick Masters anywhere. He seems to have disappeared. We're very sorry about that; I'm sure it brings you great sorrow to be without family. But you are welcome to stay here if you choose."

Jack looked at Amy. The relief that showed on her face was exactly what he felt. At least they would have a place to stay. Jack already knew what his choice would be. He wasn't about to go back to that cave under the bridge with no food and no bed except the cold hard sand.

But the general was continuing: "But there is another choice. As you know, the Barkers here have no children of their own—as much as they have wanted them. And they would like to invite you to be their adopted children and go with them to America. This is your other option. We don't want to put any pressure on you, so you choose freely to go or to stay."

Both Amy and Jack turned in astonishment to the Barkers. The Barkers were smiling. "We would like to have you," said Martha gently. "We've already come to care about you very much."

Jack just stared. Go to America? Be adopted? He opened his mouth but no words came out. To his relief he heard Amy stutter beside him, "Th-thank you, Ma'am. Thank you, General, sir. We . . . uh . . . Jack? Do you want to go?"

Jack nodded dumbly. Then a big grin spread over his face. They were going to America!

✧ ✧ ✧ ✧

Just two weeks later Jack and Amy stood on the deck of a great ship. "There's our trunk," said Jack, as they watched the last of the crates and luggage being loaded into the hold. The morning fog was lifting and

London's towers were coming into view. Jack looked over the ship's side. The dockmen had loosened the great ropes that held the ship and the sailors were hauling them on board.

"Jack, look!" Amy said, tugging on his sleeve. Jack looked up. A couple of the smaller sails had been loosened and were slowly filling with air. The ship edged away from the docks into the River Thames on its way to the sea.

The children looked around for Philip and Martha. The Barkers were standing near a pile of their belongings talking to another man and woman. A small child clung to the other woman's skirts. An older boy—maybe fifteen—and a girl about Jack's age completed the group.

"That must be the other Salvation Army family who's also going to America," Amy whispered.

"At least there's some other children on this ship. I wonder if they'll be friendly—us being adopted and all."

The word felt funny to Jack. *Adopted*. They had gone with the Barkers to the magistrate, who had asked them a lot of questions about their parents, their Uncle Sedgwick, where they had lived before and what they were doing in London. Then Philip had talked a long time with the magistrate, and Jack overheard words like, "highly irregular," and "you do-gooding Salvationists."

Then, abruptly, the magistrate motioned to Jack and Amy once more. "Do you children desire to be adopted by Philip and Martha Barker, and do you choose to go to America of your own free will?" Both children nodded firmly.

"So be it, then," the magistrate had growled, scrawled his signature on some papers and pushed them forward for the Barkers to sign.

Now as they stood on the deck of the ship, their new father interrupted Jack's thoughts. "Come on, then," Philip motioned to Jack and Amy. "Let's take our satchels to the cabin and get settled for the voyage. Martha needs some help."

The ship had moved out into the Straits of Dover by the time the new little family had made up their bunks and unpacked their things in the cramped cabin. They hadn't talked to the children from the other family yet, but the boy had nodded friendly-like at Jack and stood back so Jack could go down the narrow steps to the lower deck with his bundles.

Now he and Amy were back up on deck as the sea breeze tugged at the large white sails above them causing the rigging to creak. In the distance the White Cliffs of Dover seemed to wink and wave in the sunshine. Martha Barker stood beside them humming a tune that Jack recognized, but he couldn't remember the words. Finally, he said, "Ma'am, excuse me for interrupting, but what's that song you're humming?"

"Oh that?" she said, and she began to sing:

We're bound for the land
of the pure and the holy.
The home of the happy, the Kingdom of love.

"Is that where we're headed, Mrs. Barker?" asked Jack.

Martha smiled. "It sure is, but not on this ship. That song speaks of God's Kingdom. It is Jesus, alone, who can take us there. But we're on our way, sure enough. And just like you and Amy chose to be adopted into our earthly family, you can choose to be adopted into Jesus' family too. Then we'll be bound for that other Kingdom together."

Mrs. Barker rested her hand lightly on Jack's shoulder. He let it stay there as he looked out over the choppy blue waters. Amy caught his eye and smiled. They were heading for a new life, and, yes, he wanted to know more about that Kingdom of love.

More About William and Catherine Booth

BORN IN NOTTINGHAM, ENGLAND, on April 10, 1829, William Booth grew up learning the trade of a pawnbroker. His father died when William was just fourteen, and life got harder for the poor family. But the next year William became a Christian and soon committed his life to telling others the Gospel. William was especially influenced by the methods of the great evangelist, Charles G. Finney.

Catherine Mumford was also born in 1829, on January 17, in the English town of Derbyshire. Her parents were Methodists and took great care to give Catherine a good education. Catherine was a good student and is said to have read through the Bible by the age of twelve. She gave her life to the Lord at home at the age of seventeen.

As young people, both William and Catherine were very concerned about how much damage drinking could do to people and families. In fact they first met each other at a friend's house when William quoted a poem about the evils of alcohol. Their relationship grew over four years until they married on June 16, 1855, in South London.

Together they forged a great partnership in a traveling evangelistic ministry. Most remarkable was the fact that Catherine, in addition to William, became a powerful preacher, something women didn't do in that day.

They became particularly concerned for the poor people of England. To minister to them, they opened the East London Christian Mission in 1865. In a short time, William Booth began calling the mission the "Salvation Army." This name reflected his and Catherine's sense that in order to save people from evil and bring them to Christ, Christians needed to organize and behave like an army, the Lord's army, going into spiritual battle. Their newspaper was called The War Cry, leaders in their mission were "officers," converts were called "captives," and people began calling William, "General." Outreaches of their mission into new cities (and later other countries) became known as "invasions."

In 1881 the Salvation Army moved its headquarters to a former billiards club at 101 Queen Victoria Street, just a block away from Saint Paul's Cathedral.

The enthusiasm of this movement not only brought the Gospel to people, it gave poor people something new to live for. Even though the characters of Jack and Amy in this book are fictional, their situation was very real. The slums of East London were said to have a "gin shop" every fifth house with special steps to help even the tiniest children reach the counter. By five years of age many children were severe alcoholics, and some even died.

But the street corner preaching of the Salvation Army was so effective in converting people and influencing them to stop drinking and gambling that business began to drop off at the pubs and gin shops. In response, the owners encouraged ruffians to attack the Salvationists. In the town of Sheffield in 1882, an organized street gang—a thousand strong and known as the "Blades"—attacked a Salvation Army procession. Later that day, General Booth reviewed his "troops" all covered with blood, mud, and eggs, with their brass band instruments bent and battered and said, "Now is the time to have your photographs taken!" It showed how hard they were fighting for the Gospel. There were many such mob attacks. The incident referred to in this story about sailors firing rockets at point-blank range into a group of singing Hallelujah Lasses happened at Gravesend, on the River Thames. In 1882 alone, 669 Salvationists were assaulted and sixty of the Army's buildings were wrecked by mobs. Over the years, in many outposts around the world, Salvation Army members were actually killed by violent attacks.

As this story shows, prostitution was also a severe problem in London. The city was said to have 80,000 prostitutes in the early 1880s. Over a third of these girls had been forced by white slavers into prostitution when they were between thirteen to sixteen years old. Kidnapping and shipping the youngest, most innocent girls to Europe was very common.

The Salvation Army confronted this problem head on. They staged "rescues" (as in the case of Amy). They set up shelter homes for the girls coming out of prostitution. One home, operated by a Salvation Army sergeant, Mrs. Elizabeth Cottrill, redeemed 800 girls in three years. Finally, seeing that a main problem was that there were no laws protecting young girls, General Booth staged seventeen days of nonstop protest meetings in London and gathered 393,000 signatures on a petition that measured two-and-a-half miles long. The Salvation Army soldiers grimly marched to Parliament and demanded that the government pass and enforce new laws. This the government did on August 14, 1885.

Hunger was an equally severe problem in the slums of London. Because of the poor health conditions, orphans were everywhere. By 1872, the Salvation Army had opened five lunch rooms where—night or day—the poor could buy a cup of soup for a quarter of a penny or a complete meal for six cents. Thousands of meals were given away free.

In time, Booth realized that what the poor needed was training in new job skills and relocation out of the city. This the Salvation Army attempted in the 1890s. Urban workshops (initially safety-match factories) were set up to get homeless and jobless people employed and off the street. The next stage was to move them to colonies in the country where they could learn farming skills. Finally, they were given the opportunity to move to new settlements overseas where they could get a new start on life. While this grand plan did not last past 1906, the Salvation Army still provides effective urban workshops to help homeless and jobless people. Today the Salvation Army helps 2.5 million families around the world each year. Also, their program to help people stop drinking is the largest in the world.

William Booth used to say that he liked his religion the same way he liked his tea—"H-O-T!" By this he meant that he did not like the dull and boring kind of services that took place in most churches. The Army's banner that announces "Blood and Fire" refers to the saving blood of Jesus Christ and the fiery power of the Holy Spirit. This "hot" Gospel was one key to the Salvation Army's effectiveness. Not only did the Salvationists employ a kind of street evangelism that was more like a modern-day protest march, but Booth used music to attract people. It wasn't the somber kind heard in most cathedrals; it was lively music that stirred people up. He encouraged his musicians to write Christian words to the popular tunes of the day. And it worked. People soon began singing along, and the message got through. Even today, Salvation Army bands play on street corners at Christmas time, inviting people to contribute money for the poor.

The Booths had eight children of their own and adopted a ninth. Seven of the Booth's children became well-known preachers and leaders—two as generals of the Salvation Army. But on October 4, 1890, Catherine Booth, who had never been strong physically, died of cancer at the age of sixty-one.

William Booth continued in the ministry, traveling world-wide and preaching 60,000 sermons before he finally died on August 20, 1912, at the age of eighty-three.

Joining the Salvation Army with its challenge to take the world for Christ provided excitement and direction that attracted many of the otherwise purposeless and hopeless youth a century ago. And the Army's dramatic social work truly transformed several aspects of bleak urban life. But the heart of the Gospel as preached by the Booths called people first to repent of their sins and then surrender to Jesus Christ as Lord and Savior.

And that solid foundation has lasted. Today the Salvation Army's three million members minister in ninety-one countries of the world.

For Further Reading:

Bramwell-Booth, Catherine. Catherine Booth. London: Hodder and Stoughton, 1970.

Collier, Richard. The General Next to God. New York: E.P. Dutton & Co., Inc., 1965.

Ervine, S. J. God's Soldier: General William Booth, 2 vols. London: Heineman, 1934.
Gariepy, Henry. Christianity in Action. Wheaton, Illinois: Victor Books, 1990.
Ludwig, Charles. Mother of an Army. Minneapolis, Minnesota: Bethany House Publishers, 1987.
"William and Catherine Booth" in Christian History, Issue 26 (Vol. IX, No. 2), 1990. (The whole issue of this periodical is devoted to the Booths and the Salvation Army.)

CPSIA information can be obtained
at www.ICGtesting.com
Printed in the USA
LVOW07s1734111217
559405LV00005B/1275/P